KIMIKO CHOU

GIRL SAMURAI

Kimiko Chou
Girl Samurai

Con Chapman

atmosphere press

A Note From the Translator

The remarkable story you are about to read is truth, not fiction, but almost as interesting as the tale itself its provenance.

I was browsing in a used book store in Worcester, Mass., when I came upon a manuscript in Japanese, tied with twine; the text was mostly obscured by makeshift cardboard covers, and I asked the owner if he would remove them so that I might peruse it. I was told that what I held in my hands was a "grab bag" book, and that I could not examine it before purchase.

I was thus faced with a choice; expend $5 out of the paltry $200 stipend I would receive for my presentation on "Worcester: Unknown Tributary of the Algonquin Roundtable" at Quinsigamond Community College that night, or pass up what could be a significant addition to the study of cross-cultural currents in the literary traditions of central Massachusetts. I hoped—what a naïve young adjunct professor I was back then!—that I could persuade my department head back at the University of Missouri-Chillicothe to reimburse me if Quinsigamond C.C. did not, provided I donated the work to the school's library.

Well—never has my money been better spent, never have I taken such a leap of faith and landed so cleanly! The unbound pages were the memoirs of Kimiko Chou, daughter of Kimiko Kiyotaka, fourteenth century samurai.

When Kiyotaka left his family in 1331, he told his twelve-year-old son Tadashige, Chou's twin brother, to be brave and remain loyal to the emperor. He urged no similar counsel on his young daughter; after all, a girl could not grow up to be a samurai.

But his words of filial obligation fell like seed upon barren ground, for shortly after his father departed the boy was killed, along with his mother, Hino, by a band of thieves who broke into their home. Hino defended her family as best she could, wielding the *naginata,* a polearm, and *tanto,* a dagger that when sheathed looked like a fan, but she and her son were overcome. Only Chou survived.

The manuscript tells Chou's tale, as best as she could piece it together, from memory and the ruins of her family. I have no reason to doubt its veracity; the notion of the unfaithful narrator would not enter world literature until 1605, when Miguel de Cervantes wrote *The Ingenious Nobleman Sir Quixote of La Mancha.* Chou put her words down nearly three centuries earlier in fine *Kanji* script on rice paper, sandalwood bark, even hibiscus stalks— whatever came to hand. I am quite certain she was blissfully free of the guile that infects modern novelists of the Occident.

And so I commend this humble account—along with my occasional notes as translator—to you. There is an old Japanese saying: *"Akinasu wa yome ni kuwasuna,"* which may be translated literally as "Don't let your daughter-in-law eat your autumn eggplants." After the long and arduous task of translating her memoir, I consider Chou to be my daughter now, and I hope you will welcome her into your hearts like a daughter-in-law, and share your autumn eggplants with her.

Dr. Etaoin Shrdlu
Professor of Comparative American Literature
University of Missouri-Chillicothe

CHAPTER 1
THE BEGINNING

My name is Kimiko Chou, and this is my story. I have set it down so that it will live after me, for other girls to read. They may find it hard to believe, but it is true.

My given name "Chou" means "empress child butterfly." It was given to me at my *oschichiya*—naming ceremony. I was swathed in white, like a little cocoon, pure as I came into the world. Like every other *aka-chan* ("little red one," loving term for a newborn baby), I wore only this color of godliness for seventeen days. From then on, I was clothed in the colors of the world, and not just the pure shade of *ame*.

It should not surprise you that I came to live as a samurai, for the way of the samurai is death, and I was born, so to speak, in death. When robbers invaded our home and attacked my mother and brother, I hid in the alcove—the *tokonoma*—that is found in the main room of a samurai's dwelling, and in which is displayed a single beautiful object for contemplation. I held myself still and breathless while the robbers ransacked the house for money and weapons; they looked only for things of material value, and therefore didn't notice me. I pulled my clothing over my head like a sea urchin in order to save myself.

How, you ask, is such conduct worthy of a samurai, if the samurai, faced with a choice between life and death, must choose the latter? Well, we all want to live, and we form our thoughts according to our will. But at that moment, I was not a samurai, and I had no master. I had no aim in life, other than to survive.

When the robbers departed, I was alone. My mother, Hino, and my brother, Tadashige, were both dead. My father—Kimiko Kiyotaka—was gone, part of a force that had invaded the kingdom of Koguryo (current-day Korea). I did not know when or if he would return.

I was fearful, and for good reason. The robbers could be seen moving from house to house, repeating their acts of thievery and violence. Tada and I had recently undergone the ceremony of *genpuku,* by which we had formally been recognized as adults. I was to prepare for marriage, he was to prepare for war. I received a *mogi* (a pleated skirt), he—a samurai helmet. If I became my twin brother, I would be able to defend myself from the assaults of the robbers, and I would not be an object of attraction to them. And so I donned the garb of the samurai at an age when most girls had just begun to play the coquette. I was close to Tada, as twins will be, and so I had absorbed much of what he had learned in his training to become a samurai. Now I would become him, and adopt his name.

There was nothing left of value in our home except food, and so I cooked some rice and made *onigiri* (rice balls). These I packed into Tada's *hakama* (pants), and I set off on a quest to find my father, although I knew it might take many years. I saw myself in the eye of my mind having many adventures before we would be reunited. I would be a woman then—if I could find him before he died.

I took with me my mother's weapons: first, her *naginata*. This is a spear with a curved blade at the end. It was used by women in defending their homes when their samurai husbands were absent from the home. With its long shaft, it could be used to keep a male opponent at a distance, thus allowing a woman to fend off a man stronger than her. Next, her *tanto,* a dagger favored by women because of its short length and capacity for camouflage. When sheathed, it looked like a fan, and could concealed as an item of innocent adornment until needed. Finally, her *kansashi,* a hairpin that is a woman's weapon of last resort. Six inches long, it innocently keeps her hair in place but can be pulled out to pierce an attacker's chest or throat when he is on the point of overcoming her.

I started out on the road that led toward the sea. I wanted to go to the place where my father would land when he came back, and if that did not happen for some time, I wanted to find a way to go search for him, on a fishing boat or a bigger craft bound for Korea. I must have made a forlorn-looking sight. My brother's *kataginu* (sleeveless jacket) hung loose about my shoulders with its exaggerated shoulders, and while I tried to put on a brave face, my heart was empty—my mother and brother gone, my father far away. I was all alone in the world.

The road was a muddy path, the color of my mother's clay cooking pots. On either side were bright green hedges of grass that gave way to rice paddies. I was headed in the direction of the Tsushina Strait, toward a sky that was full of rain coming up from the sea. It was tinged with grey and blue and pink, like the inside of an oyster's shell. It was hard to be hopeful, but I tried to walk with a forceful stride, to show the world that I was determined.

After a while I heard the clip-clop of a horse coming up behind me. I did not turn to look, as I wanted to give the rider the sense that I wasn't a young girl he could trifle with, I was a samurai on a mission.

As the horseman drew nearer, he called out to me in a curt manner. "You there!"

I turned my head slowly to the left, but did not stop walking. He must know that I would not stop for anyone. He called again—"You!"

I kept walking, but said, "Yes?"

"Where are you going?"

"Korea."

He laughed. "And how will you get there?"

"I will hire a boat."

"With what?"

"Never you mind."

Upon hearing those bold words, he dug his heels in his horse's side and rode in front of me, blocking my way.

"Are you a samurai?" he asked with a mocking smile.

"I am a samurai's page."

"And who is your master?"

I hesitated just a moment. "You would not know him. He lives far from here."

"Then how did you come to be all by yourself?"

I was silent, out of words. I should have foreseen that I would be questioned, but I had not given thought to the story I would tell.

"Well?" the man asked. "Who are you, and what do you have to say for yourself?"

I fought down a lump in my throat, and spoke. "I am Kimiko Tadashige. My master is dead. I am on my way to seek my father, who is in Korea."

The man rubbed his chin, sizing me up. A boy came up behind him, dressed much like me, but in shabbier garments. I guessed that he was a page to this samurai and, from the looks of his clothing, had been traveling with him for some time. Perhaps, I thought, the man on horseback was a *ronin,* a samurai without a lord.

"I am Hyōgo Narutomi," he said with a fierce voice, as if he wanted to scare me and not just say his name. "This is my page, Moto Mori."

The boy bowed slightly and looked me over. His eyes seemed to see a rival, or even an adversary, even though I was just a stranger walking along the same road.

"I could use another page," Narutomi said with a tone of cold calculation, as if I were a fish in a market.

At first, I did not know what to say. I would be out of food soon enough, and I wanted protection from robbers and others with malice toward me.

"Where are you going?" I asked.

"The same place you are," Narutomi replied calmly, as if that settled the matter.

I looked off to the horizon behind Mori to my left, and Narutomi ahead of me. There was no shelter, and no other road to be seen, all the way to the end of the world within my view. What choice did I have, other than to continue with my concocted story about where I came from, and where I was going?

"All right," I said, without enthusiasm. "I will come with you."

CHAPTER 2
THE LIFE OF A RONIN

My new protector was a *ronin*—a fallen samurai—as I had surmised. I would learn over the coming months that he was a bit of a rascal, having been dismissed by seven lords in his lifetime. He was now looking for his eighth sinecure, and presented a bedraggled picture to any who might consider him.

"Seven times down, eight times up," was his motto; he seemed unperturbed by his current state of affairs, and went about his quest with an air that was almost smug. "If one has not been a *ronin* at least seven times," I heard him say whenever he would plead to be taken on as part of a *daimyô*, "he will not be a true retainer." This argument was not received well by those who had been loyal retainers and had served their masters. It was like the song of the crow, which is unpleasant to human ears.

Despite—or perhaps because of—all his bragging, Narutomi was a bit pathetic. I was not good at guessing ages of adults, and with his weathered face I wrongly assumed he was at least fifty. It turned out he was barely forty. With such a trail of failure behind him you would think he would be humble, but no. To hear him talk, you would think he was a great warrior. I already had my doubts.

Still, forty is not too old to be of use to a lord. In olden times it is said that men of sixty went to the front lines of battle, alongside boys as young as thirteen. As men grew older, they concealed their age so that they could continue to lead the charge. Nowadays, we have men like Narutomi, who must use an affected booming voice to impress his pages.

"Look sharp, Tada," he snapped at me, bringing me out of my reverie.

"What?"

"Your long sword—it hangs too low."

My bamboo sword had belonged to my brother, who was a few inches taller than me. It had been given to him by our father, at his *genpuku.* The problem was not that the sword was too long, but rather than his clothes were too big for me. I hitched up my *obi* (belt), and cinched it more tightly around my waist.

"That's better," Narutomi said. "You must take care always to look the part of the samurai, otherwise people will doubt you."

"All right."

"Tada?" he persisted.

"Yes?"

"You must also speak properly at all times—with

proper respect, careful diction."

I continued to walk along behind, when he stopped with a hard pull on his horse's reins.

"Tada?"

"What?"

"Perhaps you would like to answer me again?" He said this with a sneer. I glanced sideways at Mori—he was smirking, suppressing laughter.

"Yes, Master Narutomi."

"That is better," he said, then clucked his tongue, a signal to his horse to resume his trot.

"Can we stop to get something to eat?" Mori asked in a whining tone.

"We will see what the road offers," Narutomi replied. Easy for him to say—he carried in his bags some rice cakes that he would munch on from time to time whenever he got hungry.

"*Psst*," I hissed through tongue and teeth at Mori.

He turned toward me with a harsh expression. I held out one of my last rice balls to him.

He looked it over suspiciously, then glanced up at Narutomi's back.

"*Arigatou*," he said in thanks. He did not smile as he took it.

I could have acknowledged him, but thought better of it. He might have taken it as an insult, as if I *deserved* his thanks. My remark would also increase the chance that Narutomi would hear our exchange, and grow angry.

We came up alongside a peasant's hut, and Narutomi raised his hand in a grand gesture for us to stop, as if he had an army of many men marching behind him. "Halt!" he said. "We will eat here."

An old woman was tending a fire in a brazier, cooking some duck eggs, bean sprouts and wild onions. Narutomi got down off his horse and approached her in a peremptory manner.

"You! Old woman!"

The grey-haired one was stooped over, her back bent with age. She could only see us by turning her head slightly to the left. She said nothing.

"By order of the Ashikaga shogunate, I commandeer this meal for myself," he said. "And my pages," he added, as an afterthought.

The woman looked at Narutomi, a blank expression on her face.

"There—the food. It is ours! We need sustenance in our battles against the Minamotos!"

The woman stared at us, not understanding, or pretending not to understand, then spoke. "I am loyal to Ashikaga," she said, perhaps sensing that by taking sides with us, she would avoid death.

"Good—then you will let us eat our fill!" Narutomi said.

The old woman backed away, and Narutomi stepped forward. He grabbed a wooden cooking utensil from the woman's hand, and prodded the mixture with an air of aggression, singing to himself:

> *No roof but the stars above my head,*
> *I make my bed each night in the fields.*
> *Each day I prepare myself for death,*
> *Beware of the sword that I wield!*

I couldn't help but giggle, and I gave Mori a sideways glance to see if he too found humor in the contrast—a mighty samurai whose weapon was the spatula of the lowly cook—but he stared ahead stoically, a model of deference.

When Narutomi was satisfied with his efforts, he called for the woman to bring bowls for us.

"I have only one," she said, and given her humble dwelling, I had no reason to doubt her.

"Well then, we will take turns," Narutomi said. "Give me what you have."

The woman stepped inside her hut and returned with a small wooden bowl. Narutomi took the spatula and cut the food into two portions, then pushed the larger into the bowl. He ate it with his fingers, pushing the food from the bowl into his mouth rapidly, like lava overflowing the rim of a volcano. When he was through, he handed it to Mori. "You next," he said, as he lifted half of the remaining half of the food from the wok into the bowl.

When Mori had finished eating, Narutomi said to me "The rest is yours," and went off to relieve himself, leaving Mori to graze his horse in the field nearby.

The old woman looked at me with eyes that pleaded. I scooped out what remained in the wok and handed it to her. "This is yours. I am sorry for what my master has done."

Her head began to bob and tears formed in her eyes. "I can share," she said.

"No, it is yours. I have food of my own," I said, holding out my last rice ball to show her. "See?"

She thanked me, but I corrected her gently. "You do not need to thank me for what is yours."

Narutomi had returned from the woods, and called to Mori to bring the horse to him.

"We must ride on," he said loudly. "In service of our

shôgun."

He climbed onto his horse and began to saunter away, with Mori trailing dutifully behind. I turned to say goodbye to the old woman, but she had gone inside her hut, away from the greedy eyes of wandering *ronin.*

CHAPTER 3
MORI WRITES A POEM

While my new master put on the attitude of a samurai, a *ronin* is one who has fallen far from the lofty cliffs of dignity that a warrior stands upon.

Ronin means "wave man," a vagrant adrift without a home. There are two ways in which a samurai can become a *ronin,* neither of them honorable.

When a *daimyo* loses a battle, he must commit *seppuku* (ritual suicide). If his samurai are honorable men, they will follow his example. If they are not, they will look about them with selfish eyes. Their leader's lands have been taken by the victor, and their leader is gone. "Why should I do something for him," they ask themselves, "when he can do nothing for me?" It is easy for them to decide to live a life of comfortable shame, rather than do the honorable thing.

The other way in which a samurai becomes a *ronin* is to commit an indiscretion, and be dismissed by his master. For example, if a samurai is involved in a drunken brawl, or commits a breach of decorum within the castle—if he engages in petty thievery, for example—he should rightfully be discharged.

And so a *ronin,* however much he may preen and posture, is not a samurai. He roams the country as an outcast until he can find another master.

I could only guess at what transgressions against the samurai code Narutomi had committed, as his version of his history was an unbroken series of brilliant victories in the service of his past seven masters. He attributed his numerous dismissals to the jealousy of rivals, which he claimed to attract wherever he would go. That he was *not* a samurai was made clear to us for the first time one day as we passed an inn where a samurai stood outside, eating sour plums.

"Hey there," Narutomi called out in an overly-familiar tone. The samurai just looked up without speaking, so he continued.

"Help me out, fellow warrior," Narutomi said, swinging off his horse. "I am a *ronin* and these two young fellows are my pages."

At this the samurai shifted his gaze to Mori, then back up to Narutomi with indifference, as if to say "So?"

"We have been riding all day and have eaten only what we could take from an old woman," he said with a laugh. "Help us out, will you?"

I thought I detected the samurai's armor bob up and down from a stifled laugh of contempt.

"I am a warrior—like you!" Narutomi continued.

At this, the samurai grew angry. "Do not flatter yourself," he snapped. "You should be ashamed, robbing an old woman, begging on the open road. You should cut yourself open and let your guts spill out."

With that the samurai climbed up on his horse, and road away, scowling at Narutomi as he went.

"You see?" he said to us as he watched the true warrior go. "I inspire envy in the hearts of my peers. It is sad . . . seeing them so consumed with jealousy!"

Mori seemed to take it all in, eyes open wide, the faithful servant. I came to a different conclusion.

"Let's get going," Narutomi snapped at us, as if we had been the ones holding things up.

We took to the road again, our leader on horseback, while we dragged along behind.

"Here, carry this!" Mori said, tossing a *hoko* (spear) at me.

I said nothing, as was my practice. I did not want to get into an argument with him, much less Narutomi, so I accepted whatever tasks they threw my way, even though in this case my arms were already full with Narutomi's shield. I would not have minded except that, without the spear, Mori's hands were now empty. He fished his right hand into his pocket and drew out a little scroll and what looked like a little black rock, and began to scratch on the parchment.

"What are you doing?" I asked, trying to control my irritation.

"Working on a poem."

I inhaled, and turned my eyes up toward the sky. Why, I thought, does Mori get to fob work off on me while he engages in refined pastimes like poetry?

"How does it go?" I asked, doing my best to suppress a smirk.

Mori turned to look at me, to see if I was seriously interested.

"You really want me to read it to you?"

"Sure. Let's hear it—maybe it will make my heavy load seem lighter."

That jape flew right by him. "All right," he said, cleared his throat, and began:

> *Into each heart there is a winding path.*
> *Some are lined with stones, others grass.*
> *One must choose the right sandals,*
> *Otherwise one's step may cause a scandal.*

He looked over at me, awaiting my reaction. My cheeks began to puff up like a *fugu* (blowfish).

"Well?" he asked.

"I . . . I think it is good—but it needs work," I said, happy to let the air out of my lungs to answer his question, although I struggled to keep from laughing. I fixed my face into an expression of pleasantry to appear impressed.

"How so?"

"Well, who do you intend it for?"

He blushed slightly. "It is . . . to woo a girl."

"Ah!" I exclaimed, as if sun breaking through clouds had made clear something that had been obscure. "Well, good luck in your romantic pursuits."

"What is wrong with it?"

"What is the scandal you talk of?"

"There can be many scandals when a man pursues a woman."

"You are talking of boy and girl."

He grumbled a bit, then turned his eyes back to the path, as did I.

This was my first experience of the difference between men and women when it comes to poetry. Mori was so infatuated with his work that he let it fly away into nonsense. Had he kept the feet of his verse on the path of his poem, he would not have stumbled clumsily into foolishness for the sake of a rhyme.

CHAPTER 4
I AM ALMOST DISCOVERED

I was a girl, only a little bit shorter than my brother when he died, and so I could pass for a boy at least for a while—long enough, I hoped, to find my father. A *ronin* wanders without a home, and thus does not attract suspicion on the highways.

Still, I had to take constant care that I did not reveal myself as female. Samurai are supposed to be meticulous in bodily cleanliness, and although Narutomi fell short of this and many other ideals, we bathed whenever we came alongside a cool stream, which presented me with difficulties.

"Come on in," Mori said to me on one occasion, when I was unable to bathe separately because the inlet in which we washed was so small.

"All right," I said, leaving my *fundoshi* (loincloth) on.

"What is the matter?" Mori laughed when he saw me. "Don't you have any hair on your golden balls yet?"

I feigned embarrassment. "It is not that," I said, lowering my head in an attitude of shame.

"Well, what then?"

I hesitated for effect, then said softly—"Lice."

"Lice!" Mori yelled in a voice that mixed disgust with laughter—he was such a boy.

"Who has lice?" Narutomi said from the bank, where he had been lying down with his *eboshi* (black silk cap) covering his eyes while he tried to nap.

"Tada—not me," Mori said.

Narutomi removed the cap from his eyes and propped himself up on one elbow to look. "Is this true?" he said to me.

"Yes."

He laughed a little, a contemptuous laugh. "This is a hazard of the samurai," he said with the gravity of one learned in the ways of the warrior. "But I have something for the little *shirami,*" he continued, referring to the lice.

He stood up and went over to his horse and began to dig in a bag that was fastened to his saddle. This was his *kubibukuro,* which samurai use to carry the severed heads of their enemy. Since Narutomi had never prevailed in battle, he used his for odds and ends. He dug around inside it for a while, then pulled out what looked like a piece of fur.

"Try this," he said as he approached me.

"What is it?"

"Underwear from the skin of a badger."

"*Anaguma pantsu!*" ("Badger-pants!") Mori yelled in that annoying teenage boy voice of his.

"Quiet, Mori. This is a defensive move. The fight is won before the battle if one is prepared. In a long campaign, lice are troublesome."

"Thank you," I said, not taking off my pants.

"Put them on," Narutomi commanded.

"In a little while—let me dry off first."

He dropped the furry undergarments on the bank and walked back to where he had been resting before and lay down again.

"I won't be sharing my clothing with *you*," Mori said as he got out of the water.

"I wouldn't want your clothes."

"Well, I certainly don't want *yours*."

With that he got out and rubbed himself dry, and I was able to emerge from the water and change into the badger-skin pants out of the view of the man and the boy. I do not know what Narutomi would have done had he discovered that I was a girl. The daughter of a samurai is taught chastity from childhood, but instruction in this principle comes with many subordinate teachings that are far removed from its foundation. Keep a distance of at least six feet from men, my mother told me. Do not look them in the eye, she said, do not take anything directly from their hands. What these have to do with chastity I do not know, and in any case, how was I to find my father except by entering the world of men in disguise?

When Narutomi woke from his nap, he felt the urge to exercise—or more precisely, to direct his pages to exercise—so he found sticks of bamboo about the length of *katana* (long, single-bladed swords) and set us to fighting, using a two-handed grip.

We circled each other warily at first, then Mori swung

at me with a wide, swooping motion. This left him exposed when he missed, and I jabbed him in the side with my weapon.

"Easy, Mori," Narutomi said. "It is better to land a single fatal blow than a thousand mosquito bites."

Mori was bigger than me. If I was to defeat him, it would have to be by tactics, not strength. I kept my distance, forcing him to lunge at me if he wanted to make contact. I could thus see him coming, and adjust my response accordingly.

I tried to lure him into rushing me, with some success. While a running start gave added force to his blows, it allowed me to step aside at the last second.

"Come on, fight!" Mori said finally as he became frustrated.

"I am, but I am not required to suffer your blows!"

"Tada is correct, Mori," Narutomi said, appraising us from the side. "You must triumph by your mind as well as your body."

We continued in this vein for some time, Mori coming at me with sword upraised, me jumping outside his range as he came close enough to strike, then hitting him on the back. Finally, exasperated, he turned on me after one of these cat-and-mouse maneuvers and dropping his sword, wrestled me to the ground.

"Get off of me," I yelled, my voice cracking as if I were about to cry.

"You do not fight fair!"

"Enough for now," Narutomi yelled, pulling Mori up by the shoulder. "We must be off again on our *musha shugyo*" (warrior pilgrimage). He saddled up, and we followed behind.

We passed that day on the road in silence, Mori and I. It had taken only the slightest frustration for his mistrust and resentment of me to break through to the surface from its hiding place in his heart.

CHAPTER 5
OUR DESTINATION

I have made light of Narutomi, but I must give him this: he wanted to become a samurai again, and not remain a *ronin*. He, like I, was on his way to Korea, where he hoped—he said—to join in battle against that nation's Righteous Army. He was confident he had something to contribute—perhaps he only wanted to share in the spoils of war that others would win, but could not carry. "They are a ragtag band," he said one night as we sat looking into the fire. "No match for samurai."

"Like my father," I said, revealing for the first time the reason for my journey.

"Your father is a samurai?" Narutomi asked. Perhaps I should have kept silent.

"Yes. I am going to Korea to find him."

"Perhaps," Narutomi said, rubbing his chin

thoughtfully, "I can join him . . ."

He allowed his voice to trail off, and looked slyly at me.

"I don't know," I said, not wanting to promise him anything.

"I would be a valuable addition," he said and popped upright, striking a pose with his sword.

I nodded, but kept quiet. My slip of the tongue had turned out to have value, like a coin found along the road. If Narutomi wanted to become a samurai again, and my father was a samurai, then he needed me, and would get me where I wanted to go—Hirado, a city on *Jīng hǎi* (Whale Sea, the modern Sea of Japan), from where I could take a boat to the battlefields of Korea.

I glanced at Mori, and saw that he was looking at me through narrowed eyelids. If one of us was dismissed it was now likely to be him, who had before held precedence.

We took off the next morning, continuing our journey to the sea. The city of Ōita was the only life I had known. My world was expanding, like the rings that proceed outward when a pebble is tossed into a pond, but the object that had disturbed my tranquility was the murder of my mother and brother; unlike a pebble, not a slight thing.

We had made it as far as Yufuin in our journey, and arrived in the cool of the evening to hear the ringing of the temple bells. Off in the distance was Yufu-dake, with its snow-covered peaks.

"Can we climb it?" Mori asked.

"What for?" Narutomi asked contemptuously.

The question puzzled Mori. "To see from the top," he finally said, his face twisted up in an expression of consternation, as if to say: "Why else?"

"What you see from up there is what you see down here. We cannot stop to gaze at every pretty vista we pass."

"But I want to!" Mori said.

"The way of the samurai," Narutomi began, and Mori and I exchanged looks of annoyance. "Here we go again," Mori said as he rolled his eyes.

". . . is death. We must prepare ourselves for death every day, by meditating upon the many forms it may take. Impaled by a spear. Pierced by arrows. Swept away by a great wave. Struck by lightning. Shaken to death by an earthquake. Falling from a thousand-foot cliff . . ."

"Climbing a mountain could help us meditate on that," Mori said, excited to have trapped Narutomi in a blind alley of his own thinking.

"You can contemplate it down here," Narutomi said, cutting off the discussion. "We are not monks seeking to withdraw from the world, we are samurai! We are nothing if we do not do battle with the world!"

"Where shall we stay tonight?" Mori asked. "I am hungry."

"We will go to one of the temples; they will feed us and give us shelter."

I waited for Mori to point up Narutomi's contradiction—one minute we were warriors, scornful of monks, the next we turned to them for aid and comfort. Mori said nothing, however. Perhaps he had had enough of arguing with a mind that was changeable as the wind.

Narutomi stopped at the first temple we saw, and told us to wait outside while he secured the monks' assistance. We sat on the temple steps and watched as he pleaded our case with a mixture of unction and bluster. He bowed low in unison with the monk who came out to deal with us, then asked "Shukubo?" Meaning, he wanted to take advantage of rooms available for visiting monks and pilgrims.

"You are not a monk," the man who had emerged from the temple said. "Are you a pilgrim?"

"Oh yes, quite," Narutomi said.

"Where are you going?"

"To Korea."

"And what for?"

"To . . ." It dawned on Narutomi as he began to speak that a monk would not favor a warrior who planned to invade another country. "To, uh, carry the principles of Buddhism to the natives of Korea."

"Buddhism *comes* from Korea," the monk replied.

"Really?"

"Yes. From Baekje. We are members of the Soga clan— we brought the way of Buddha with us when we came here from Korea. So there is no need for you to take the Eightfold Path there—that is where it came from."

"Ah," Narutomi said. "Perhaps I was misinformed. Well, in any event, we need food and lodgings for the night."

"We?"

"Me and my pages there," Narutomi said, indicating by a sweep of his arm Mori and me.

The monk looked at us with more sympathy than he had shown to Narutomi. "All right," he said. "You may stay one night, but you must follow our rules."

"Oh, surely we will."

"We close the gates early, there is a curfew."

"This is fine, we are tired from our long day's ride."

"You may join us in meditation if you—or the boys—

wish."

"I may do that," Narutomi said with a smile that Mori and I had never seen on his face before. It was—I don't know how else to say it—a smile that hid a lie.

We spent that night among the monks, but we did not—as Narutomi had suggested—join in their meditation. "Who has time for that?" Narutomi said contemptuously. "One must be a man of *action* to succeed in the world."

Mori and I exchanged glances. "Look at this temple," Mori said, indicating by a sweep of his arm the very large shelter in which we would spend the night. "It looks like they do pretty well for men of inaction."

Narutomi emitted a snort, like a horse. "I suppose begging is a form of action, but I personally am above it."

"What have we been doing on our way here?" Mori asked. "I would call it begging."

Narutomi's eyes narrowed—I was afraid Mori had gone too far. "It is not begging to take what is rightfully yours due to your place in society. We are warriors—we take what we need to sustain ourselves, so that we may defend our *daimyo*—and everyone in it."

The explanation seemed a convenient excuse to me, but I was not about to challenge Narutomi. Mori had been traveling with him longer than I, and his familiarity had both jaded him *and* emboldened him.

We shared the monks' food that night, and I was grateful for it. It was the first full meal I had eaten since leaving home.

CHAPTER 6
WE LEARN OF THE WAY

We took to the road again early the next morning. The monks made it clear, in their subtle way, that our stay with them had come to an end. They were up and about with the dawn, busy with their chores, while Narutomi snored away. Finally, Mori gave him a poke.

"Whuh?" was the sound he made.

"It is time to get up," Mori said. "They have given us some food to eat on the road."

"They—who?"

"The *monks*. They don't want us hanging around."

Narutomi slowly came back from whatever dream world he had been visiting, and sat up. "Well, *that's* not very hospitable."

"They have fed us—twice."

"Still, if I were them, I'd be careful."

Mori suppressed a laugh. "Why?"

"Because if you do not do good in this life, in your next life you are reborn as an animal, or a hungry ghost." Narutomi saw a monk walking across the open room where we had slept and began to speak in a louder voice that he pretended was not meant for the monk's ears. "I'd hate to think of what kind of low beast a man would come back as if he threw poor pilgrims out of his temple after only a one-night stay."

The monk did not even turn his head in our direction, so Mori and I continued to roll up our blankets and prepare for a long day on the road, while Narutomi continued to grouse to himself.

We made good progress once we left the temple, our bellies full and our bodies rested. We stopped only briefly when the sun was high overhead at noontime, to get out of the heat for a while and water the horse. We ate the remains of the food that the monk had given us, then were on our way once again. When we stopped for the night, it was already getting dark and a light rain was falling. We made camp in the mouth of a cave, where we would be sheltered from a greater storm if one came. Narutomi sent Mori and I off to gather firewood before the woods were wetted.

"The teacher is as a needle," Narutomi said to us as Mori and I started the fire to cook our evening meal, "the disciple is as thread."

"What does that mean?" Mori asked as he snapped a stick in half, making a cracking sound that echoed the sharp tone in his voice. He was annoyed at the mundane nature of the tasks we were required to perform each day.

"It means I am the . . . uh . . . hole through which you

must go."

"To do what?" I asked.

"To uh, complete yourself."

"Thread doesn't have to go through needle," Mori said. "You can use it to tie things up."

"Yes, but if you want to sew you must—thread the needle."

"I don't want to sew," Mori said. "I want to be a samurai."

Narutomi looked up from his . . . it wasn't actually work, but he made it seem as if he was doing something useful by whittling a reed with his short "companion" sword.

"If you wish to broaden your spirit, you must pay attention even to trifles," he said, then pursed his lips and nodded, as if admiring the pearl of wisdom he had found in the clamshell of his skull.

"But . . . haven't you also told me 'Do nothing which is of no use'?" Mori asked.

"Well, yes."

"So . . . there is not much difference between a trifle and something that is of no use. How are we to tell the difference?"

I could hear Narutomi grumble in his throat a bit. He didn't appreciate this challenge to his authority, even if it was cloaked in the form of an innocent question.

"You do not know the difference because you are not a samurai," Narutomi said. "When you know the difference, you will be a samurai."

Mori grunted, barely making a sound, but I heard him. He was chafing under the tedium of chores, but someone had to do them. If I had not been with Narutomi, I would have been at home with my mother who would also have set me to work on domestic duties. Mori, on the other hand, saw himself as a warrior-to-be. If Narutomi had been a real samurai, his *daimyo* would have employed many women to perform menial tasks, and Mori could have spent more time learning The Way of the short sword and the long sword.

I had not started out to become a samurai, only to find my father, but every day I became more intrigued with the life that my father had chosen to lead, and The Way that Narutomi spoke so much of even if he followed it so imperfectly. What was this "Way"? How did one find it? Where did it begin and where did it lead?

The fire was burning now as the green sticks of spring had hardened in the month of *Satsuki* ("early rice-planting month"—May). We ate our rice and Narutomi drank his *sake* (rice wine).

"Narutomi?" I asked.

"Yes?"

"What is . . . 'The Way'?"

The flames cast a glow of dancing figures on his face, and his eyes took on a dreamy cast. He began to speak in a faraway tone of voice.

"The Way is . . . *the way.*"

"That doesn't tell us much," Mori said.

"For a samurai, there is no other way *but* . . . The Way." Narutomi said this with a tone of finality, as if to cut off the relentless questions of a teenager.

"But what *is* The Way?" Mori persisted.

"The Way is . . . the path we are following," Narutomi said. "For you to become samurai, and for me to be restored to my rightful place as faithful retainer to a *daimyo* who can support me in the style I once enjoyed."

Mori poked at the fire with a stick. "You told us that if we wanted to follow the way of the samurai we must meditate daily on death," he said. "You seem to spend all your time thinking about how to have a more pleasant life."

"What did Shida Kichinosuke say?" Narutomi asked with a learned air. Mori and I shrugged our shoulders—we didn't know.

"When there is a choice of either living or dying, as long as there remains nothing behind to blemish one's reputation, it is better to live," Narutomi said. "I have lived a blameless life, so I . . ."

"But you told us seven times you have been dismissed," Mori said.

"Over trifles," Narutomi said. "Never was I faced with a choice between dying and not dying. Sometimes I was simply odd man out. Not enough armor to go around, that sort of thing." He picked at his teeth with a piece of straw, affecting a superior air. Then, perhaps as strategy to evade an opponent who had cornered him in conversation, he spoke to me. "How about you, Tada? Do you truly want to become a samurai, or are you just along for the ride?" He said this with a smile, looking to me as an ally who could help him.

"I . . . think I do," I said. "It is a long and difficult process—correct?"

"Yes."

"With no assurance that I will find a sinecure, and not become a wandering *ronin* such as you?"

"That is true, but adversity strengthens you."

Mori snorted just a bit, a sound of contempt, but I sat

between him and Narutomi and thus served to shield the source of the noise.

"What was that?" Narutomi said, a challenge to Mori.

"It must have been Piebald," Mori said—Narutomi's horse.

Narutomi peered around me at Mori with a look of fierce skepticism, like a teacher who will punish an entire class rather than let one miscreant get away with disrespect.

"Then perhaps you should go lead him to water," Narutomi said. "The rain has stopped."

"I will go with you," I said, tired of parrying my master's thrusts. As pages, we were only allowed to groom and feed the horse, not take him out on our own.

"Don't go far," Narutomi yelled as he leaned back on the *kubibukuro* he used as his pillow and closed his eyes.

Piebald had a large head, a drooping back and a friendly gaze. His white coat was dotted with patches of color, one of which resembled a *Fenghuang,* the bird that reigns over all the others. He stood five feet, four inches high, but his best days were behind him—according to Narutomi, he was twenty years old. As a result, it was easy for me and Mori to keep up with him as his gait rarely exceeded a walk.

"Let me ride him," I called out to Mori, but he was up onto Piebald's back before I caught up with them.

"You can ride him on the way back."

We headed back to a stream we had seen late in the day. It ran alongside the road, forming pools here and there where there was a depression in the ground, or where stones blocked its path. "He can drink here," Mori said, as he climbed down and led Piebald by the reins to a little puddle. The horse had different ideas, though. He lifted up his head and looked into the woods, as if he sensed something there.

"C'mon, boy," Mori said. "We haven't got all night."

Piebald snorted, and tossed his head. I turned my head to see what troubled him, and saw nothing—just the movement of the sky pencil holly bushes waving gently in the breeze.

"It is all right, Piebald," I said as I rubbed his withers, but he jerked at the reins violently and when I turned around I found myself facing two men in fearsome samurai armor. They towered over us with their helmets, and their short swords were drawn.

"Whose horse is this?" one of them asked.

"It is our master's," Mori said.

"Why are you out on the road at night?" the other asked.

"The horse was restless, we took him to find water," I said.

"All horses on this land are the property of our *daimyo*," one said.

Mori drew himself up, "striving for height" as we had been taught by Narutomi, and he drew his sword. I didn't know what he was thinking—*if* he was thinking. The two men had swords of *tamahagane*—jewel steel—while his was made of bamboo.

"Ha!" one said when he saw Mori's attitude of battle. "You are just a boy—do not force us to kill you—surrender the horse."

"Never!" Mori said. I backed away as the men stepped forward. One grabbed Mori's weapon from his hand and grappled with him, the other grabbed Piebald's reins.

"Stop!" Mori screamed, but the man grasped him more tightly until he could not speak.

The other man examined Piebald, pushing back his gums to look at his teeth. He bent over to look at his spavined hock joint. His aspect was that of a man buying a horse, not seizing it as plunder. "Let him go," the man said.

"Why?"

"This horse is not worth taking. It would be more trouble than its value."

"But . . . we have orders."

"We do not have orders to do something foolish. This horse is not suitable for eating, much less feeding."

The other man released Mori from his grasp. "Continue on, you may not stop here. This is the land of Lord Shima," said the man who made the harsh appraisal of Piebald.

"We can stay as long as we want," Mori shouted, and the man who had held him slapped him hard, across the face, knocking him down.

"Go on with you, leave," the other said.

The two men turned and receded back into the woods, as silently as they had come. I looked down at Mori and thought—such a foolish boy! To stand on pride when nothing was at stake.

"Are you all right?" I asked as I bent over him.

He touched his hand to his cheek. He was bleeding, but not badly. It had been a blow of contempt for a youthful opponent who dared to oppose a samurai, and was not intended to have mortal consequences.

"I guess."

"Let's get moving—they may be watching us."

"All right."

I climbed up on Piebald and made a clicking sound with my mouth. He took off at his usual ambling gait, and we headed back to our camp. When we arrived, Narutomi was asleep, snoring loudly.

"Should we wake him?" I asked Mori.

"Why should we?"

"Because of the men—they told us to leave."

"I don't care. I am tired and hurt. I want to sleep."

And so he lay down in the warm night. Just moments before he had been ready to fight a man with two swords. Now he was curled up in a ball, like a little boy at the end of a busy day at play.

I looked at him, and at Narutomi. I decided we could take a chance that Lord Shima's retainers would not pursue us. If they had wanted to take Mori and me, they could have--they didn't even want Piebald. We were a minor irritation, like a burr under a saddle, not a threat.

I joined my fellow "warriors" on the ground, in their very pacific posture of sleep.

CHAPTER 7
A BELATED ALARM

When I awoke the next day, I did not at first remember what had happened the night before, perhaps because I had not been harmed and thus the encounter was of little consequence to me. Mori still slept, perhaps still feeling the effects of the blow he had taken to his head. Narutomi had a fire going, and didn't seem happy that he had been forced to do the chores that were the responsibility of his subordinates.

"Good morning," he said in a gruff voice as he stirred a pot of rice. "I do not recall your return last night—where did you two go?"

"Oh," I said, as I remembered what had happened to us. "We were set upon by retainers of the *daimyo* whose land we are crossing."

"Hmph," Narutomi snapped. "An unlikely story."

Mori groaned, and rolled over. He put his hands to his face to block the rising sun.

"Up with you!" Narutomi shouted, and when Mori did not respond, he stood and went over to rouse him. "Now!" he said, as he grabbed Mori's arm and flung it aside from his eyes. "What happened to you!" he exclaimed when he saw the purple eye and scratches Mori had received.

"I told you—two men came out of the woods and detained us," I said. "One of them hit Mori when he resisted."

A new mood came over Narutomi, one that I could not decipher. He was at first incredulous. "Is this true Mori?" he asked.

"Yes, but I am fine. They were each two-sword men."

Now Narutomi turned wary. "Did they follow you?"

"No, but they told us to get out of their master's fief."

"Why didn't you wake me?" Narutomi asked, now full of bluster.

"Mori collapsed when we got back," I said. "I made the judgment that they were unlikely to follow us. They went back into the forest after they examined Piebald and found him not worth stealing."

Now Narutomi bristled with resentment. "My horse was not good enough for them?"

"You should be glad of that," I said.

Narutomi looked off into the distance, as if to see if he could spy the men who had decided we weren't worth the trouble. "How far is the place where they accosted you?"

Mori was sitting up now, rubbing his one good eye, gingerly touching the other.

"Not so far," he said. "Out of earshot from here, just over that rise."

Narutomi scratched at his stubbly face. "I wonder if Lord Shima could use another retainer," he said, his egotistic thoughts escaping from his mouth without seeming effort on his part, as if they had tongues of their own.

"They didn't even want your horse," Mori said. "Why would their master want you?"

Narutomi wheeled on him and snapped "He will have heard tales of my prowess. My reputation in battle has spread far and wide."

I watched the two spar but kept silent. Mori seemed emboldened by his first taste of combat, even if he had been easily vanquished by a grown man. Like many arguments, this one produced no light for all its heat. Finally, when Narutomi seemed about to overrule Mori as a simple brute expression of his status over us, I chimed in.

"I do not want you to join Lord Shima's men. I am on a quest to find my father, so I must go on to the sea. If you stay here, I will have to leave you."

Narutomi looked back and forth between the two of us, his young cadets. His face lost its put-on expression of gruffness, and he appeared to engage in an inward calculation. What would he be with an aged horse and no retainers? A diminished man, for sure, and he needed to buttress up his current edifice to appear a worthwhile acquisition to a *daimyo* of any consequence as it was.

"All right, we will continue on," he said. "I would not want to be one of Lord Shima's retainers if that means I have to chase children like you who stay up past their bedtimes."

That settled that, and we ate our breakfast and packed

up for the day's travel. When Narutomi began to mount Piebald, the horse balked. I thought the horse was skittish from its night of conflict, and told him so.

"He was handled roughly by the retainers last night," I said. "Perhaps it would be better to go gently with him today."

"What is a samurai without a horse?" Narutomi snapped as he tried a second time to mount Piebald, but again the horse shied away.

Mori and I looked at each other. Our fortunate escape seemed to have created a harmonic resonance between us. We were no longer rivals, or whatever we had been yesterday. We were comrades in adventure.

"You should let one of us ride him," Mori said. "He needs to start out small again, and become refreshed."

Narutomi made a noise like a bullfrog in a bog, a sort of "harrumph." It would be a fatal blow to his pride if he were to be seen walking while one of his pages rode, so Mori's suggestion presented him with a conundrum.

"I will break him again," he said but again Piebald reared and would not be mounted.

"Let us try," I said.

"Fine," Narutomi said, then walked off a few steps to watch.

Mori looked at me. "You try first, you are lighter."

The reins hung down loosely from Piebald's bridle. I looked at him, and decided to stand where I was for a moment and watch him. He snorted, and looked back at me. Was this an invitation, or a challenge?

"Piebald," I called out in a voice that I tried to disarm. It was not a command, nor did I scold him. I simply tried to convey that I wanted to talk to him.

He stood where he was, pawed the ground once, and tossed his head. I began to approach him in a roundabout way, as if mounting him was not on my mind.

I made as if I wanted to inspect the grassy area that Piebald had turned his nose up at the evening before. I pulled some *kanto* (dandelion) and brought it back to him.

"Here is something you missed," I said, holding it out to him. He noticed the bright color, and lowered his head to nibble.

"No, this is a treat," I said softly, teasing him a bit by pulling the plant away from him. "You must work with me, like last night."

He snorted, and waggled his head.

"All right, you may have it," I said and allowed him to eat. "That's my good boy," I said. "Now may I have a ride?"

He whinnied a bit. As gently as I could, I stepped into the stirrup and hoisted myself up. He didn't flinch, and allowed me to climb into the saddle, where I sat while he finished the dandelions. I turned and looked at Mori, who gave me a nod of appreciation. Narutomi looked a bit put out. "It looks like you ride, and I walk," he said. I clucked my tongue, turned Piebald onto the road that led us on to the sea, and the others followed.

CHAPTER 8
PIEBALD BECOMES A DEITY

I brought Piebald around to his old self through gradual and gentle persuasion, and within two days he again allowed Narutomi to mount and ride him. Once that happened, I was demoted to walking with Mori. My return to the humbler mode of travel had one advantage; I could again confide in Mori and swap stories, which my position on horseback precluded.

"Do you know what Narutomi did to become a *ronin*?" I asked Mori one day when Piebald, startled by a rabbit bolting across the road, had uncharacteristically broken into a trot, and put some distance between him, Narutomi and us.

"Which time?" Mori asked facetiously, and we both laughed.

"The most recent—or any of them."

"One can lose the rank of samurai for a number of reasons."

"Like what?"

"It is never anything serious, otherwise his *daimyo* would have ordered him to commit *seppuku*. It is more of an . . ."

Mori hesitated as he searched for the word he wanted.

"A . . . breach of decorum?" I offered hesitantly.

"Yes, such as getting drunk, or brawling. Or making a gross noise at table."

"Narutomi must be an extremely crude man to have been dismissed so many times."

"It could also be that others excelled him in skill, or in obsequious praise of their lord."

"I find the first to be more likely than the second," I said. "His tongue is gilded for flattery."

"It could also be that a turn of bad fortune came, such as a bad crop of rice one year, so that the lord could no longer support all his men."

"If that happened, he would not dismiss his most valuable retainer—would he?"

"No," Mori said, and smiled at me in recognition. We both knew that our master was not an estimable man, but he was the one that fate had cast in our way.

"You two—stop dawdling!" Narutomi shouted from the road ahead, turning Piebald around to look at us.

"You go too fast!" Mori said, but we hastened to catch up a little.

When we were once again alongside Piebald he neighed at me. "He wants to stop," I said to Narutomi.

"Oh, so now he talks to you?" Narutomi said, one eyebrow lifted in skepticism.

"He is easy to understand if you listen to him," I said, and made a clicking noise with my mouth. Piebald tossed his head as if to agree.

"All right," Narutomi said. "If you two are in charge, we will do what you say."

"Thank you," I said. We pulled off the road into a pasture of tall grass. Narutomi got down, and Piebald headed off to graze, with me holding on to his reins. I tethered him, and came back to where Mori sat alone.

"Where is Narutomi?" I asked.

"He went off to relieve himself." We knew this meant he would be gone for a long while, and it was at this time, out of our master's earshot, that I learned Mori's story.

"Are you Narutomi's son?" I asked, as blandly as I could.

"No."

"How did you come to follow him?"

Mori looked down at his hands for a moment, then off into the direction where Narutomi had wandered.

"I ran away from home," he said. "I wanted to become a samurai, but I could not. My father was not a samurai, not even an *ashigaru* (foot soldier). He was just a peasant."

I saw that Mori was embarrassed by the lowly stature of his family. "So—what has Narutomi promised you?"

"That he will lead me along the path. I will become a warrior through his training, and then when he becomes a samurai again, *I* will be eligible—like you."

I had an advantage by birth over Mori. As the apparent son of a samurai, my way was not impeded by obstacles that blocked his path. Perhaps this was why Mori tolerated me, and had even become friendly toward me. There was unfortunately nothing I could do for him, or for myself.

"I think it is unlikely that Narutomi will become a samurai again," I said. "He is old and slow, like his horse."

"He is my only hope."

We quieted ourselves as we saw Narutomi coming. He hurried across the field with unusual haste.

"The men you saw the other night," he said in a hissing whisper as he got nearer. "What did they look like?"

"We couldn't see them well," Mori said. "It was dark, and they wore helmets."

"There are two horsemen on the crest of the hill you see beyond that rise. I don't think they saw me."

"What shall we do?" I asked.

"We must evade them, and if we cannot, we must appear harmless," Narutomi said.

I looked at Mori—he looked at me. We stifled laughter, but Narutomi noticed.

"Why do you laugh?"

Now Mori could hold it no longer. "An aging horse, two youths, and you. I don't think we present a threat to mounted warriors."

Narutomi stepped forward and, sooner than the time it would have taken for Mori to see it coming, slapped him.

"You will never become a warrior if that is the way you think," Narutomi said. "I have a retinue and a horse. I am as qualified to be a samurai as they."

"Then we must take steps to disguise our fierce nature," I said, hoping to defuse the conflict.

"How?" Narutomi asked.

"We will become as monks," I said.

Narutomi scowled. "Who would believe that?"

I thought for a moment. "We will all sit down, and

chant. If they approach us, we will ask for alms."

"Monks don't usually own horses—do they?" Mori asked.

"No, but we will tell them Piebald is . . . sacred."

We could hear the sound of hooves off in the distance—there was no time to lose. "Piebald!" I called out as I ran to him.

He lifted his head from the tuft of grass he was eating. I untied his reins from the tree branch where they were secured, and in a hushed voice said "Lie down." He did as I told him to. "Lie still," I said as I stroked his mane, and touched the mark that set him apart from other horses.

"Sit around him," I said to Mori and Narutomi. "Like this."

I crossed my legs in the meditative manner of a monk, let my eyes roll back into my head, and began to chant. *"Na Mo Tat Sa Pha Kha Wa,"* I began, although I did not know what it meant—if anything. It was just something I had picked up by ear.

"We will not fool them—we are not monks!" Narutomi snapped.

"Sit!" I hissed and, after glancing over his shoulder, he obeyed. Then Mori, following his lead, joined the three of us on the ground.

"Like this?" he said, as he brought his legs in close to his body.

"That will do," I said. "Now, repeat after me. *To A Ra Ha To Samma Sam Phut That Sa."* We must have made a strange sight to the eyes of the approaching warriors—a horse, a man, and two youths, sitting beneath a shade tree, reciting sutras—or what I recalled, imperfectly, as sutras. I did my best to ignore the men as they drew nearer. After all, if I was lost in contemplation of the Eternal Buddha, earthly things would be beneath my notice. Narutomi and Mori followed my lead, and why not? They had had a failure of the imagination at a most critical time, in the face of grave danger.

The men stopped at a respectful distance. The only sound we heard from their direction was the heavy breathing of their horses, winded from the fast pace of their approach.

I repeated my pseudo-sutras several times, then—out of ideas—I brought our chant to what seemed a natural conclusion. I looked up at the men and, with an attitude of beatific indifference, greeted them.

"Peace to you."

It was perhaps a misstep on my part, as the horsemen expected the eldest in the group to speak. For the first time, a look of suspicion crossed the men's faces, like the shadow of a cloud scudding low across a field.

"Who are you, and what are you doing in the fief of Lord Naohiro?" one asked in a gruff tone.

"We are monks, on a pilgrimage," Narutomi said, belatedly assuming the character of our leader. His explanation was a perfectly plausible one, but the man persisted in his questioning.

"There are no pilgrimages on the island of Kyūkoku. Where are you going?"

"Uh, we are going to Shikoku," Narutomi said.

"Then you are going in the wrong direction," the other horseman said. "You are heading where the sun sets, not where it rises."

"Why does a monk have a sword?" the first asked, looking at Narutomi's long-bladed weapon, which he had been unable to conceal within his clothing.

"Please pardon us," I said, interrupting in the hope of preventing Narutomi from talking us into more trouble. "We are not worldly men. We must travel deceptively, as we are in the presence of a deity." I nodded at Piebald, then looked back at the man with an expression of deep piety.

"A horse is a God?" the first horseman asked, with the air of one scoffing.

"Yes—come see," I said.

I stood up and beckoned to the men to examine Piebald. One dismounted, leaving his reins in the hands of his partner.

We drew closer, and I pointed to the firebird patch on Piebald's coat.

"Ah!" the man exclaimed. "So I see. Kizuka!" he called to the other.

"What?"

"Ride and tell the clan to provide safe passage to these monks."

"I cannot."

"Why not?"

"I am holding your horse."

"I mean *after* I take my horse."

"Oh."

The man named Kizuka handed the reins to his partner, then rode off. "He will carry word of your coming, you will not be molested while on Lord Naohiro's land."

"We are grateful," Narutomi said, nodding his head over his hands folded in prayer.

"I will accompany you to the next *sekisho* (guard station), and tell them of our good fortune in having you traverse our fief."

"Lead the way," Narutomi said. "Can one of my pages ride with you?"

"Certainly," the samurai said, and Mori got up behind him.

The horseman turned his steed onto the road, and we prepared to follow him. "This is an important lesson," Narutomi said to me as he mounted Piebald and helped me up.

"What is that?"

"The great samurai Yamamoto Tsunetomo said fish will not live long where water is clear. If there is duckweed, they can hide under its shadow and thrive."

"What does this mean?" I asked.

"Deception is a weapon when you have no sword."

But . . . you did have a sword, and it was I who conceived the plan of deceit, I thought, but did not say. We were out of danger, and that was all that mattered, not who got credit—as between him and me—for our successful strategy.

CHAPTER 9
NARUTOMI LOSES HIS LONG SWORD

It took us the rest of the day to traverse Lord Naohiro's land. The samurai who escorted us showed us the way to go through the bordering *daimyo,* then he asked us for our blessing. Narutomi played the part of the priest, and Mori and I his acolytes.

"May you become at all times, now and forever," Narutomi intoned, "a protector of those without protection." He inhaled, and looked back upon the land from which we had come. "A guide for those who have lost their way, a ship for those with oceans to sail. A bridge for those with rivers to cross. A sanctuary for those in danger, a lamp for those stumbling in the dark." Again, he paused. I had to admit, for someone whose daily habits had not previously revealed any interest in sacred things, he was putting on a good performance as a holy man.

He took one final deep breath. "May you be an ass to bear the burden of a heavy load up the hills of life, and a servant to all."

"Thank you," the warrior said, in a tone of humble obeisance.

"Now, would you like to make an offering to the Avatar?"

The samurai dug inside his kimono, pulled out a bag full of coins, and handed it to Narutomi.

"We thank you, and the Buddha thanks you," Narutomi said, bowing his head.

"Safe travels," the samurai said, turned his horse around and, with a wave of his hand, rode off.

We waited until the horseman was far out of earshot, then we could contain ourselves no longer. We all broke out in laughter at the same time, like a firecracker exploding.

"To hell with the high-born and their stupid retainers!" Narutomi yelled. Normally he hid his bitterness over his low station from us, but having gulled a samurai out of money, he was so pleased he couldn't restrain himself.

I suppose I should have felt at least a slight pang of guilt, but I did not. Perhaps I was becoming just as bad as Narutomi, or maybe life on the road had caused my moral faculties to wither. Mori laughed even harder than me— perhaps I would one day become so callous that I wouldn't even reflect on my duplicity.

Now that we had money we could pay for a meal for the first time in many days. We rode until we came upon an inn, a modest-looking establishment with two horses tied up outside. We went in and Narutomi, feeling flush with the success of our gambit, called for fish and rice in an expansive tone, then added: "And bring me a bottle of *sake*!"

Two men sitting on the floor at a low table looked over at us, sizing up Narutomi in particular. I thought it unwise of him to speak so loudly, with such an air of boastful prosperity. It could only attract unwanted attention from highway men, and even a party of two brigands could overpower a man, a boy and a boy-girl.

Mori and I ate in silence while Narutomi expounded on The Way of the Samurai, a subject about which he loved to hold forth even if he was a seven-time failure in this field of endeavor.

"You two, you must remember the lesson of this day," he said as he put a piece of fish in his mouth with his chopsticks. "You must be ruthless in worldly matters, so that you can feed the body." It would have been unwise for me to point out that it was Narutomi who wanted to run from Lord Naohiro's retainers—both because it would have made Narutomi angry and because it would have alerted the two men to the soft belly beneath his brittle shell.

Narutomi went on in this vein, his indirect praise of himself growing with each sip of sake. "Young men should discipline themselves in courage—it must be fixed in your hearts," he said between bites. "If your sword is broken, you must fight with your hands. If your hands are cut off, you must push the enemy down with your shoulders. If your shoulders are cut, you must butt him with your head. If your head is slashed, you must bite him with your teeth. This," he said dramatically as he completed his litany of desperate measures, "is what courage is."

"Excuse me," we heard a voice say. It was one of the two men, who had been watching and listening, and had gotten up and come over to our table.

"Yes?" Narutomi said with a mixture of formality and deference as he inspected the armor that the man was wearing.

"I couldn't help but overhearing you speak of the Way of Samurai. I found it very instructive. Are . . . you a samurai?"

"Right now, I am a *ronin*, I go back and forth," Narutomi said with a reflective tone. "I like the security of being a retainer, but I also enjoy freedom."

"I understand completely," the man said. "I am at my master's beck and call for his every whim. It is," . . . here the man looked around, as if to assure himself that there was no unknown man of his master within earshot . . . "a dog's life."

"I hear you," Narutomi said, nodding his head.

The other man got up and joined his companion at our table.

"This is Akechi Mitsuhide," the first man said. "My name is Sanada Yukimura."

"Our master is a good man, but he is too cautious," the one named Mitsuhide said.

"Caution is a problem for a samurai," Narutomi said. "We must act on instinct, otherwise we are lost."

"This is true," Yukimura said. "We train for many years, but must be ready to act in the time it takes for a snake to shrug its shoulders."

Narutomi laughed at the figure of speech in a collegial sort of way, a fellow member of a fraternity of fighters.

"Are you an expert swordsman?" Mitsuhide said.

"Well," Narutomi began, affecting modesty like a *saburuko* (serving girl), "I *have* achieved a certain degree of skill."

"Ah," Yukimura said. "It would be good to receive a demonstration of your technique."

"Yes," Mitsuhide added. "Would you perhaps be willing to show us a few of your favorite cuts?"

Narutomi stroked his chin as if considering whether he should reveal valuable secrets to men he'd just met. Then, with an air of magnanimity, he said "Sure, let's go outside and I'll show you a few tricks."

Narutomi tossed some coins on the table, hitched up his belt by the hilt of his sword and we went outside.

"What I am interested in learning," Mitsuhide said as he drew his sword, "is the tactic I have heard of called The Flowing Water Cut."

"Ah!" Narutomi said as he gripped his sword. "This is a vital tool in close-arms fighting." Mitsuhide approached as if to get a better look at Narutomi's hands, and Yukimura took a stance behind Narutomi, as if to observe from that angle.

"Grip your sword like this," Narutomi said, and before I realized what was happening, I saw Yukimura drop to his knees and Mitsuhide push Narutomi over him, using his sword as a battle staff. Yukimura sprang up, grabbed Narutomi's sword and stood over him, while Mitsuhide brandished his long sword at Mori and me, keeping us away.

"You are not so expert with the long sword as I supposed," Mitsuhide said. "Your skills are not equal to your annoying boasts."

"Please do not take my long sword," Narutomi

pleaded.

"Ha—so this is the fierce warrior who has been regaling everyone with his tales of glory!" Yukimura said, then added "Stay where you are!" when Narutomi put his hands on the ground and started to get up.

Mitsuhide untied the men's horses from a tree and brought them over to where Yukimura was standing. The two mounted, turned their horses onto the road and galloped off.

"Let's go after them!" Mori said, but Narutomi just sat there.

"On Piebald? I don't think so," he said. He slowly rolled over onto his hands and knees and got up. "I am one pathetic samurai now. No armor, no long sword, and a swayback horse that couldn't catch a turtle."

As bedraggled as the four of us—horse and three humans—looked before, the picture we presented to a curious eye was even worse now. A *ronin* without a sword; a horse on aged legs; a boy, and a girl disguised as a boy. For the first time in a while, I felt discouraged.

"What shall we do?" Mori asked.

"I don't know," Narutomi said. His native—or perhaps foolish—optimism seemed to have deserted him. He plopped himself down upon a large, smooth, white stone and exhaled, a bit winded from the rough handling he'd received from the two highwaymen. "If we stop now, we have nothing. If we continue on to the coast as we'd planned, there is a chance I can catch on with a lord who needs troops for battles with The Righteous Army of Korea. If I stop and turn around, I go back to . . . nothing."

"But . . . I thought you taught us that the *Ni To Ichi* way of strategy was the spirit of the void, and that the void is nothingness," Mori said.

"That I did, but that is a different kind of nothingness."

"How can one nothing be different from another?" Mori asked, with relentless adolescent logic. "There is nothing in nothingness, and since there is nothing, it must be all the same."

"No, the nothingness of failure is bitter. The nothingness of the void is virtue."

"I don't see how this can be," Mori said. "Nothing is nothing is nothing."

I sensed that it was not a good time to annoy Narutomi, but Mori seemed oblivious. "Let us ride on," I said after watching this standoff of the male minds I was stuck with. "I must find my father, you two wish to win glory on the battlefield. We have no other choice, so let's stop arguing fine points of philosophy."

Narutomi pursed his lips and nodded in agreement. "Yes, let us carry on—after we finish our meal." He hoisted himself up with difficulty—he must have been hurt in the scuffle—and began to walk back toward the inn. "You have spoken wisely, Tada," he said to me. "We are like sharks, we must keep moving forward at all times, otherwise we die."

Mori looked at me with a scowl. I was afraid I had slid backward down the hill of friendship I had climbed with him, but I had no choice. Every moment that the men dithered was a loss of precious time for me. My father might be killed before I ever saw him again, or he might advance so far in the campaign into Korea that I would never find him. I did not have the male luxury of idle disputation.

CHAPTER 10
IN SIGHT OF THE SEA

We still had some money, since the men who had robbed Narutomi only took his long sword, perhaps assuming from our bedraggled appearance that our pockets were empty. We were thus able to keep our bellies full for the next few days. We took turns riding Piebald—Narutomi had been humbled enough by circumstances, and Mori and I had grown enough in his eyes through our mastery of his lessons, however shoddy they may have been—that he began to treat us as his helpmeets and not his inferiors.

I had fashioned a bow from a *karasu-no-sanshō* (crow prickly ash tree), and arrows from a *yanagi* (willow tree), and began to practice archery. It required strength to pull the bow, but also calm. When Mori shot arrows they flew farther than mine, but I was more accurate than him.

Perhaps it was that teen-boy impetuousness that I often noticed in him. Narutomi had neglected his bow-and-arrow skills in his long period of wandering as a *ronin*, and was worse than either of us.

"Archery is good as strategy out in the open, when you fight army against army, but what use is it when you are in hand-to-hand combat?" he said. "Your adversary will cut your head off in the time it would take to draw your bow."

"We no longer have your long sword, just bamboo, so it is something to do," Mori said. "*And* it will help us to eat. You cannot kill a *usagi* (rabbit) with a short sword." Despite Mori's posturing, it was me, not him, who was better at hunting game. In addition to rabbits, which made good stew, I also shot *risu* (squirrels). I had tried to shoot *kamo* (ducks) and other birds out of the air, but I was not yet good enough. We also ate plenty of fish, which we caught with a hook and line, and *kame* (turtles), which we could snatch up with our hands.

Narutomi had become wary of the people we met after our experience with the two samurai he tried to impress in the inn. I almost felt sorry for him. What is the use of being a braggart if you are too scared to lie to people? He needed to open himself up like a flower every morning to feel good about himself. Instead, he hid his personality, like grasshoppers you find underneath a log in the morning. I could tell that it was wearing on him.

"How long before we reach the Whale Sea?" I asked him one night before the fire, as we ate our meal of rice and a small bird Mori had stoned with a makeshift slingshot.

"I would say"—here he looked off into the sky, as if that

helped him to calculate—"four days, maybe more." I was pretty sure from the lack of confidence with which he said this that he had no idea, but still wanted to seem in command of our little ragtag band.

"Do you think any of your . . . prior masters are fighting The Righteous Army?" I asked tentatively. I thought he might have a better chance of catching on with someone he had served in the past.

"Perhaps," he said, tossing a bone into the fire.

The way he said it suggested to me that it would be harder for him to be retained by someone who had known him, not easier. I had to keep his spirits up, for if he lost faith in our mission, I would have to find some other way to get to Korea. He may have been a proud, vain and boastful man when I first met him, and a broken man now, but he was my only hope.

We went to sleep that night under clouds lit from behind by the moon. Narutomi tossed fitfully in his sleep, perhaps fighting his assailants again in his restless mind. For the first time I felt pity for him.

When we awoke we continued toward the Whale Sea, stopping briefly in the morning to let Piebald eat in a pasture of *zoysia* (grass). Our stomachs growled but we rode on, as we had spent almost all of the money that Lord Naohiro's samurai had given us. "Perhaps we should try our monk trick again," I muttered to Mori as we walked behind Narutomi on Piebald.

"I doubt it would work again," Mori said. His spirits were low as well, made worse by the emptiness of his belly. "As we draw near the coast, we will need to be better actors than out here in the tall, uncut grass."

"I would shave my head to look like a monk," I said.

"It is not just our hair. The people who live near the coast are not as gullible as country types, they would see right through us. We need to come up with a new ruse."

We walked in silence for a while. I looked off into the green field, trying to come up with an idea by indirection. Sometimes my mind works that way. Leave a subject that puzzles you and come back to it, with your mind refreshed. It did not work this time, however, and we walked on in silence.

We saw a farmhouse off in the distance with *chabo* (chickens) out front. An old man steadying himself with a pole was taking feed from a bag strung over his shoulder and sprinkling it on the ground, which the chickens pecked at. Narutomi turned his head to the right to look at them—I knew what he was thinking: to take by force that which he had no right to, simply because he was hungry and desperate. He no longer had his long sword, however, so I wondered how he planned to do it.

"Hey there, old man!" Narutomi called out in a gruff voice. It is a samurai tactic to shout in order to disturb the enemy. Narutomi had instructed us in the use of the voice as a thing of life, to show energy at the beginning of a battle.

The old man looked up and stopped his feeding.

"Yes, you!" Narutomi continued. "We hereby declare one of your chickens to be . . . uh . . . spoils of war and property of Lord . . ."

Here Narutomi turned to us with a cupped hand and asked, "Whose land were we crossing back there?"

"Shima," Mori said.

"No, that was before," I said. "It is Naohiro."

"Right," Narutomi said, then turning back to the old

man, shouted "Naohiro!"

The old man bowed low, his hands clasped together in obeisance. "In that case, come and take one of my chickens," he said.

Narutomi turned to us, his lips pursed in an expression of smug self-satisfaction. "I guess I can still command respect when I have to," he said under his breath.

Narutomi dismounted and approached the house confidently. "I am pleased that you have chosen to submit to his Lordship's mandate," he said as he drew nearer. "I will be sure to tell my Lord of your humble obedience to his will."

The old man smiled, bowed again, then waved his hands toward the fowl. "Take whichever one you want," he said, but when Narutomi stepped forward to do so, the old man stuck his staff between Narutomi's legs, tripping him. With Narutomi on the ground, the old man proceeded to beat him, raining blows on his head and arms.

"Ow! Stop!" Narutomi cried, but the old man would not relent. He poked his staff in Narutomi's groin, fully disabling him for the time being. Narutomi groaned miserably.

"Get off my land and never come back!" the old man snapped. "You two!" he shouted at us. "Come get this cur and take him away."

We approached warily as the old man glowered at us, brandishing his pole.

"Oh!" Narutomi groaned.

"Take him by one arm, I will grab the other," Mori said. I did as he said, and we dragged Narutomi back to Piebald.

"How are we going to get him up on it?" I asked.

"We won't be able to," Mori said. "We will have to make a *sori* (sled) to pull him."

"How will we do that?"

"We will find some long sticks, bind them over Piebald's back and at the other end. We can stretch a blanket over that frame, and Narutomi can ride in it."

Mori's plan seemed too complicated to me, but I went off to look for pieces of crow prickly ash or willow we could use to make the device he had described. I climbed up to the top of the rise where there was a stand of trees and began to search on the ground for sturdy pieces of wood— I found three, then began to look for a fourth. The forest was dark but not deep, and I could see to its far edge. As I walked through it I smelled not just the scent of bamboo and ferns and evergreens, but something new. I inhaled deeply through my nostrils—what was it?

And then I realized—it was salt from the sea! I walked with hurried steps to the point where the forest ended at a field of yellow grain and looked—blue water!

I turned and started to run back to the road. "Mori!" I shouted.

"What?" he yelled back.

"We have made it—the Whale Sea!"

CHAPTER 11
GOODBYE TO PIEBALD

Seeing and smelling the ocean are not, of course, the same as being there. We still had to get Narutomi and Piebald and ourselves overland to the place where a boat could take us to Korea. We had left the first curled up in a ball on the ground, and the second was slow of hoof, so Mori and I would have to lead the next leg our journey.

When I returned to the road, however, things were looking up—a bit. Narutomi was now sitting up, his hand on his groin, moaning but apparently recovered somewhat from his most recent loss in battle. I presented the long sticks I'd collected to Mori, but he held up his hand in refusal.

"I think he's going to be all right," he said, and then softly, so Narutomi didn't hear. "His pride was wounded more than his nether parts."

"Ow—that bastard!" Narutomi groaned.

"Do you think you can get up on Piebald?" Mori asked.

"If you two hoist me, yes," Narutomi said, "but I will have to ride side-saddle. I cannot lift my leg over."

Mori gave me a look with pursed lips—I knew he was suppressing a laugh at our once fearless leader, now forced to ride like a woman. Had he known I was a girl, and had been matching him step for step the entire length of our journey, perhaps he wouldn't have found the reversal of roles so amusing.

"C'mon, lift me," Narutomi said. Mori and I drew near as Narutomi backed up to Piebald and held the reins. Narutomi placed his left foot in my cradled hands, then his right in Narutomi's. He grabbed hold of the pommel of the saddle with his right hand, and placed his left on my head. "On three," Narutomi said.

"One . . . two . . . three!" we said in unison.

Piebald's age and lack of mobility were, for once, advantages. He didn't bolt or buck at Narutomi's weight or the odd means of ascent. We got Narutomi positioned none too securely, but good enough for a horse that moved no faster than Piebald.

"Back in the saddle!" Narutomi said with a wince. "C'mon, let's head out!" he called to us with a game face.

We picked up our few belongings, packed what we could in Piebald's saddlebags, and headed out, trailing Narutomi riding not gallantly like a samurai, but daintily, like a lady out for an afternoon promenade to view cherry blossoms. No matter how much he still imagined himself a valiant warrior, he no longer looked the part even to an unworldly eye.

We rode for half a day before we reached Hirado,

where boats and sails crowded the waterfront. The fishermen were busy unloading their catch at the docks, and we went to an inn to eat with the last of our money.

"We will find someone here to take us to Korea," Narutomi said as he tied up Piebald up outside.

"Who will transport us for free?" Mori asked.

"I am going to sell Piebald," Narutomi said as he motioned to the innkeeper.

"You can't sell Piebald!" I blurted out with emotion.

"Why not? He's my horse."

"But . . ."—I struggled to find words of persuasion— "He saved our lives from the samurai!"

"That may be. He has served us well, but now we must travel by boat. We cannot take him."

Hearing this, I became silent. If Piebald stood between me and my father, I had only one choice.

"Did I hear you have a horse for sale?" a small, wizened man sitting at the table next to us asked.

"Yes," Narutomi said, narrowing his eyes in a way that he must have thought made him look like a sharp bargainer.

"Did he really save you from samurai?" the old man asked.

"That he did. He is courageous and loyal—he has the heart of a warrior."

The old man nodded. "May I examine him?" he asked.

"Certainly—he is right outside." And with that, Narutomi and the old man went out to bargain over the horse who had served us so well, and whom I had grown to love.

"Do you really think he will sell Piebald?" I asked Mori.

"If we want to get to Korea, he must—we have no

choice."

I stared glumly ahead as the innkeeper brought us bowls of rice and *suimono* (clear soup). I ate in silence, wondering about Piebald's future. The old man seemed like a kindly sort, but would he work Piebald too hard? He could not know of what we had been through together, how I had learned to communicate with him better than the others. I would be losing not just a horse in this sale but also a friend.

When Narutomi came back in, he had a smile on his face and was holding a *tankō,* the armor worn by foot soldiers on their chests.

"What did you get for Piebald?" Mori exclaimed like a heartless fool, as if a living, breathing horse could be replaced by mere chattels.

"I got enough for us to sail to Korea, *and* I will arrive outfitted as a warrior!"

"Let me see it!" Mori said breathlessly as he ran his hands over the iron plates.

Narutomi gave him the armor, a smile of satisfaction on his lips. He made a show of counting up his money, then called out to the innkeeper for a bottle of *sake*. When it arrived, he sipped at his drink and looked about him with a calculating eye, apparently trying to figure out which of the men in the room had a boat we could hire for passage to Korea.

"You there!" he called out to a man gulping down a piece of fish.

"Yes?"

"Are you headed out fishing?"

"Tomorrow morning," the man said.

"I am looking for passage to Korea."

"I am only going as far as Tsuikai-koku," the island in the middle of the strait.

"That will do for now," Narutomi said. "We will find another boat for the second half of the trip."

"How many?" the man asked.

"Me and my two pages."

The man looked off into the air with an expression of mercantile appraisal, named a price, and Narutomi agreed.

"Fine," Narutomi said as he poured some coins in the man's hands.

"I am spending the night here," the man said.

"So are we."

"I leave early in the morning."

"Have them wake us if we are not already up," Narutomi said, and the man walked off after nodding his agreement.

We sat there in silence for a while, now upon the threshold of our great adventure. Mori was still stroking the armor like a little girl fondling a doll.

Narutomi's face took on an expression of satisfaction, as if he had accomplished something great by his succession of swaps—horse for money and armor, transport for money.

"What will the old man do with Piebald?" I asked.

"Oh, you know," Narutomi said with a dismissive air. "Whatever you do with a horse that old."

"And what is that?" I asked.

"They make them into glue," Mori said, not taking his eyes off the armor.

"What?" I cried out.

"I suppose that's what will happen," Narutomi said,

leaning his head back to look at me straight on.

"How could you!" I screamed. "He was sacred."

"He was not sacred," Narutomi said.

"Yes he was!"

"He was a horse like any other."

"No he was not—he understood me!"

Narutomi snorted with contempt. "A horse's lot is to be born, work and die. Nothing more."

I felt myself start to cry, and I pursed my lips together to stifle my tears. Mori looked up from the armor and saw me welling up. He started to laugh at me, but stopped when I flashed him a look of fury. I did not feel like being trifled with, and I showed it.

Narutomi asked the innkeeper where we could sleep. We were directed to a room at the back of the inn, and Narutomi and Mori stood up to go there. As they left the room where food was served Mori turned back toward me.

"Are you coming?"

I inhaled a second, to steady my voice. "Not quite yet," I said, and could not keep myself from sniffling. "In a minute, when I'm done," I said as I looked down at my empty bowls.

I looked out the window, where the waterfront was visible. The sun was setting into the water, and the little fishing boats were silhouetted against the brilliant orange light and the blue-pink sky. My mother and my brother were part of the life I'd left behind, and now so was Piebald, a good horse and one I imagined I could talk to. I wondered if he had taken his place among the other *Fenghuang,* up with the celestial bodies in the sky.

CHAPTER 12
MY SECRET IS DISCOVERED

The rooms where we were to spend the night were small, so we would sleep in close proximity to each other for the first time in months. While we were on the road we slept under the stars, or if it rained, under whatever overhang we could find. Now, we were thrown together in a rectangular-shaped room that looked out on the water, and a smaller square-shaped space without windows. Of course, Narutomi claimed the big room and promptly fell asleep on a low bed, while Mori and I curled up in a corner toward the interior of the house, which was warmed by the *irori* (sunken hearth) and kitchen on the first floor. We had only one blanket, which we draped over us. I fell fitfully asleep, tired from our long journey, but anxious about our voyage the next day.

From time to time I would be woken by Mori's snoring,

or his tossing and turning, but I would roll over and ignore him, and soon would be asleep again. As the first light of dawn began to glow from the room where Narutomi slept, however, I was disturbed by movement and heavy breathing from Mori. I could feel his hand moving under the cover and finally, irritated, I turned to him and said "What are you doing?"

"What do you think I'm doing?"

"If I knew I would not be asking you."

"*Jii koi o suru.*"

I did not understand what he meant. "You . . . console yourself by rubbing?"

With that, Mori laughed out loud. "I beat off! Haven't you ever done that?"

I didn't want to appear inexperienced in the eyes of this older boy, so I said "Sure, lots of times."

"Well, then you know. C'mon!" he said as he grabbed my badger pants and started to pull them. "Show me what you got!"

He had exposed my groin before I could react, and then he just . . . stared.

"You are . . . a *futanari* (hermaphrodite)?"

"What does that mean?"

"Half boy, half girl?"

I pulled my pants back up and shushed him with a finger to my lips. "No, I am a girl," I said in a whisper, hoping Narutomi would not hear.

"But what . . ."

I told him the woeful tale of why I had left my home, and the desperate circumstances of my apprenticeship to Narutomi. "You see, I had no choice but to join you two if I wanted to see my father again." He looked at me with what I felt—for the first time ever—was pity. "You will not reveal my secret?"

He gulped, and his lips quivered a bit. "You have put me in a difficult position," he said. "To remain silent is to betray the confidence I have earned from my master."

"I know. I understand. You were Narutomi's first page, if I must leave and go back now, I will."

He looked down at his hands, then at me again. "I will not tell," he said. Then he leaned forward and gave me an awkward hug. "We need you."

"Thank you," I said. "I will not be a burden."

We sat there for a few moments, looking at each other, then we broke into embarrassed little smiles. "Now, if you don't mind, I need to go wash myself."

He slipped off like a lizard, his movements swift, silent and secretive.

I lay back down and closed my eyes. What, I wondered, was this magical rubbing by which Mori had consoled himself? I could not ask him, for to do so would reveal my ignorance. I rolled over toward the wall, turning my head away from the growing light of the dawn, and fell asleep.

CHAPTER 13
NARUTOMI'S FORTUNE IS TOLD

"Tada—wake up!"

As I heard these words, I felt my shoulder being shaken, and I opened my eyes to see Mori standing over me.

"What?" I said, still half asleep, or more.

"It is time to go."

I sat up and saw Narutomi coming up the stairs, wearing his armor. He wore something new as well—a samurai helmet, which made him look somewhat ridiculous. Apparently, the sale of Piebald had yielded enough money for him to be fully outfitted for the first time since I had met him.

"The boat's leaving, Tada," Narutomi said with the gruff aspect of a commander. The hardness of his warrior's gear had apparently penetrated to his personality. He was no longer the crestfallen victim of an old man with a stick, and the two men who had robbed him at the inn.

"Okay, coming," I said and jumped up.

The other two were making their way down to the dock as I rushed out the door. The boat Narutomi had hired for us was a small fishing vessel with a single sail. It would take us a long time to reach the island stepping-stone to Korea.

"Do you know anything about sailing?" Mori asked me nervously as he helped me into the boat.

"No."

"Don't worry, I can sail a boat this small by myself," the fisherman said. "Just stay out of my way."

Mori and I sat down in front of the mast, while Narutomi sat in the stern and talked to the fisherman as we sailed. "What kind of fish do you catch?" he asked.

"*Ayu*," he said (sweetfish). "Tuna, mackerel, sea bass. Whatever is biting."

Narutomi nodded his head knowingly. "It must be nice, living your life peacefully on the sea, instead of constantly fighting battles as I do."

"Are you a samurai?" the fisherman asked.

"Yes."

"Then where is your long sword?"

Narutomi shrugged his shoulders and made a little grimace with his lips, as if this was a minor matter. "I was set upon by a band of marauders who stole it."

"Really? How many?"

"Six . . . no, I guess it was seven counting the leader."

"You stood no chance against odds like that. How will you arm yourself again?" the fisherman asked as he looked at Mori and me, indicating with a nod of his head and a little scowl that the three of us were unlikely to overpower many opponents.

"I am going to Korea to fight The Righteous Army. My lord will supply me with a sword, I have everything I need but that," Narutomi said, and the fisherman fell quiet as we tacked into the wind, coming about from time to time as we made our way toward Tsuikai-koku.

The fisherman cast his net for bait fish when the wind died down for a while, but he had no luck. He pulled a spoon worm—it was as long as his hand—out of a bucket and hooked it onto his *gyeonji* (fishing pole). He began to troll as the wind picked up again.

"Do you know the other names for that worm?" Narutomi asked with a sly look on his face.

"No," Mori said.

"One is 'fat innkeeper.' You want to know the other?"

Mori shrugged. "I guess."

"Penis fish," Narutomi said, then started to giggle.

Mori and I rolled our eyes at our master. So much older than us, and yet as immature as a little boy.

"Ha ha," Mori said to Narutomi with a sarcastic air. Narutomi moved to the back of the boat to handle the tiller—he could not hear us with the wind blowing, and the fisherman didn't care, so we were free to talk again.

"He is so irritating," Mori said.

"I know, but it can't be for much longer."

"Why is that?"

"Soon I hope to be reunited with my father."

"How will you find him?"

I looked off at the horizon, where there was no sign of land. "I don't know—but I must."

The fisherman caught several flounder, then a few sea bream. The wind picked up so the fisherman took over the tiller from Narutomi, and we began to make good time. We sailed running free before the wind for the better part of the afternoon, and we ate one of the fish that Mori had cleaned. By the time we were finished, the sun was setting behind the island that was our destination, giving it an aura of gold as we approached it.

"It is a glorious sight, a good omen," Narutomi said, his eyes narrowed and a smile on his lips. From his expression, he seemed to face the coming battle—if he found one—with anticipation. We struck the sail as we neared a dock and an old man grabbed the mast and guided us to a post where he tied the boat up.

"Thank you," Narutomi said as we got out, but the fisherman—who was already unloading his catch to sell—merely grunted. We were cargo he was hired to haul—it was just a business exchange to him.

"How are we going to get to Korea?" Mori asked as we walked towards the little village that lay along the shore.

"Same as we did before," Narutomi said. "Now that I *look* the part of a samurai, it should be easy to find someone willing to carry us to the mainland."

The few structures that made up the settlement presented a pitiful picture. There was a one-story building that had an official look to it—perhaps the offices of the little prefecture that the island comprised. There was a store of some sort—not open. And there was a tiny inn, one that could not have contained more than two rooms to let. The fishermen who lived on the island must have had their lodgings further inland.

An old woman had made a fire on the beach, and was

cooking fish in a pot. It smelled savory, and Narutomi—of course—made a rather haughty overture to her. "Hey there, old woman!"

The woman simply looked our way.

"We are hungry samurai, going to fight The Righteous Army. What is that fish you are cooking?"

The woman spoke slowly, and softly. "It is a baby shark."

Narutomi laughed. "How did an old woman like you catch a shark?"

"It washed ashore, still alive."

"Well, we need to eat. Let us have some."

The woman hardly stirred.

"You heard me, give it up—we are starving!"

The woman took a bowl and filled it with the fish soup, then handed it to Narutomi.

"Ah," he said as he sipped it.

"What will you give me?" the old woman asked.

"What do you want?" Narutomi responded.

"I don't know where my next meal is coming from."

"Well, go down to the beach, maybe you will find another shark tomorrow," Narutomi said with a contemptuous smile, then turned to Mori and me expecting us to laugh at his jape.

When Narutomi finished, he handed the bowl back to the woman and said, "One for each of my pages!"

The woman complied, with Mori going first. When he was done, I looked in the pot and saw that there was barely enough for the woman herself. "You finish it, I ate some fish earlier today," I said.

When Narutomi heard me say this, he scowled at me. "You will never learn to be a warrior if you allow yourself to be cowed by an old woman." I was silent—the old woman simply nodded her head to me in gratitude.

"Well? Are you going to take it or not?"

"She can have it."

"Then *I* will eat it," Narutomi said, but as he started forward, I stepped between him and the old woman and stopped him.

"Let her be!" I said as forcefully as I could. He raised his right hand and slapped me with the back of it, causing me to fall backward and almost into the fire. His blow hurt me because of his *tekō,* the "gloves of hell." I put my hand to my face as Narutomi stood over me. I thought: his samurai armor has gone to his head.

Narutomi continued to berate me, as was his custom, calling me all sorts of names, a failure, a disgrace to the Way of the Samurai. When he was done, he looked over and saw that the old woman had finished her soup, and was staring at him with an enigmatic expression on her face.

"If you will give me nothing for your food, I will give you something for nothing," she said.

"And how is that, old woman?"

"I was a fortune-teller in my younger days, and I will tell your fortune for free."

"Hmph," Narutomi snorted. "And what is my fortune?"

"A shark has filled your belly tonight," she said in a flat, uninflected voice. "You will fill a shark's belly someday."

Narutomi bristled at the ominous suggestion and, before he turned to go to the inn, he kicked a little sand in the woman's direction. "That is what I think of you and your fortune-telling," he said as he stormed off.

As I said, the inn was small but it was adequate. The three of us huddled in a single room, with a single bed. I had no desire to share the more comfortable accommodations with a man who had just struck me, so I lay down on a pallet on the floor, and Mori and Narutomi slept together. I had had a long day under the hot sun, my face buffeted by the strong winds in the Sea of China. I fell right to sleep, and dreamed of another sea journey to come.

CHAPTER 14
FISHING FOR SHARKS

When we woke the next day, we set about to find a boat to take us on to the mainland. My cheek still smarted from Narutomi's slap, but I was consoled by the thought that I had only one step left—so I thought—in my quest to find my father.

The innkeeper made us a breakfast of duck eggs, and Narutomi gave me a few coins from the change he received. "Here, Tada," he said as he tossed them on the counter. "To make up for last night. I did not mean to hurt you, but I could not allow your impertinence to pass without response in front of that old woman."

"What difference did it make that she heard?" I asked.

"It . . . now see, there you go again," Narutomi replied. "Just as I submit to the will of my lord, so you and Mori must submit to *my* will. I cannot allow you to be insubordinate, at least not until you can defeat me in battle."

"At that point, I will no longer be subordinate," I replied quietly but firmly, although I doubted I would be able to overcome Narutomi's superior size and strength until he became much older.

We went down to the water to see if we could find a boat traveling to Korea, and had no luck at first. The fishermen had already left, even before the sun came up over the water. There was an official boat that brought mail to the island, but it was returning to Japan. The only craft that appeared to be free was a long wooden work boat with a foredeck that extended from the mast to the prow. In it, a man was cutting up salmon for chum. Narutomi approached him and, in his typically obtuse manner, began to talk without salutation.

"Good day for fishing, eh?"

"Yep."

"You headed out?"

"Soon as I'm ready."

"Which way are you going?"

"Into the waters off Korea."

"Ah—that is where we are headed as well."

The man did not respond to Narutomi's implicit solicitation.

"Do you think we could accompany you?"

"As what—ballast?"

"Ha," Narutomi laughed. "No, I mean, we are looking for passage to Koguryo."

The man looked Narutomi up and down. "Do you have any money?" he asked.

Narutomi gave me a look as if to say "Hold your

tongue." He stuck his hand in his pocket and pulled out a few silver and copper coins. "This is all I have," he said, as he held his palm out for the man to inspect his offering.

The man screwed up his mouth and made a grumbling sound, but then relented. "All right," he said. "You can help with the work."

"Thank you," Narutomi said and motioned for Mori and I to join him down at the water's edge. "These are my two pages," he said when we presented ourselves to the boatman, who looked us over with a gimlet eye, then allowed a sly smile to creep across his face.

"Have you ever fished for shark before?" the man asked.

"No," Mori and I said.

"Well, you will learn. Sharks are not as bad as people say."

"They're not?" Mori asked, incredulous.

"No. You can even tame a shark and ride it, if you feed it and it comes to trust you."

Mori and I looked at each other in disbelief. My thought was that the man was a wizard, and kept sharks as his familiars.

"Get in, let's go," the man said, and we followed his directions. "Push us off," he said to Narutomi, who got behind the boat and, with some difficulty, eased it off the sandy bottom with the help of an offshore wind and climbed aboard over the stern while we were still in shallow water.

"You can catch sharks with guile as well as aggression," the man said as we sailed out of the little inlet. "The sharks here know me, but they forget what I have done to their departed mates."

He let his eyes wander over the water from time to time as we made our way toward the northern end of the island, using the *Kuroshio* (black current) to push us. We made good time, and soon we were in a position to tack toward Korea.

"Get your heads down!" the fisherman called to us as the boat came about into the wind. Mori and I ducked successfully under the boom and the sail swung over to the leeward side of the boat. "These are good waters for shark," he said, "and this is their feeding time."

"I will scout for them," Narutomi said, and he climbed up on the foredeck, keeping one hand on the mast at first, then letting go when he had his balance. "I could stand to eat another bowl of that old woman's soup," he said as he spied out over the waters for the telltale fins.

The fisherman turned the boat up into the wind, causing it to stop. The sail luffed noisily, but he ignored it, and began to toss chum into the water. A shark approached and came to rest alongside us as the fisherman dropped pieces of salmon in the water. The shark ate them calmly, as if it was eating at a fish vendor's cart on a city street. The fisherman reached down with his left hand and stroked the shark's back, then eased it closer to the boat while continuing to feed it with his right hand. As the shark swallowed one particularly large piece, the fisherman picked up a gaff, hooked it into the shark's body and pulled it up against the boat's gunwale, holding the gaff down with his right leg. Then, with one swift motion, he pulled a knife from his belt and slit off the shark's fin, dropped it into the boat and twisted the gaff out of the shark's body with no more effort than it would take to remove a hook from a carp's mouth.

"Good one," he said as he threw the shark fin into the hold of his little boat.

Mori and I had watched this display of proficiency with amazed looks on our faces, as if we were witnessing a conjurer perform a magic trick.

"Wow," Mori said. "You did that so quickly!"

"You learn by doing," the fisherman said.

I looked over the side of the boat at the now-finless shark. "Is that all you take?"

"I have only a small boat," the fisherman said. "I can't carry a whole school of sharks with me back to shore."

"Don't people eat the rest of it too?" Mori asked.

"They prize the fin for soup, and do not care for the rest," the fisherman said as he again took hold of the tiller and turned to steer us farther out into the strait.

I looked at the shark, which was floating on the surface, listless, losing blood. "What will happen to him?" I asked.

"He will sink to the bottom," the fisherman said. "He can't swim without his fin."

"So . . . he will just die?"

"Yes. That is the way of the world. One thing dies so that another might live."

I looked back at the shark as we sailed away. Its dark back was scarred by a streak of red and, as the fisherman had said, it seemed to have lost both the will and the ability to swim.

"Will other fish . . . eat it?" I asked.

"Perhaps," the fisherman said. "Who cares—it is just a shark. If it had its way, it would eat us."

I looked out over the water and saw the fin of another shark, perhaps attracted by the blood of the one whose fin we had taken.

"There are a lot of them over there," Narutomi said to the fisherman, pointing off to the port side of the boat, and indeed a swarm of four or five sharks had begun to swim alongside of us. "Let me help," he said, as he grabbed the fisherman's gaff.

"Hold on," the fisherman said, "I'm coming about." The boat turned to the left as the fisherman pushed the tiller to the right, and we were in the thick of a school of hungry sharks. Narutomi slid his hand down the mast and extended the gaff over the water.

"Not like that," the fisherman said. "You must be patient."

"All right," Narutomi said, as he stood up again, still holding on to the mast.

"Let me turn up into the wind again." The fisherman turned his boat head-on into the wind blowing off the strait, slowing the boat to a stop, and Narutomi let go of the mast. He looked out of place in his armor, gear more appropriate for battle, not fishing, but—like a beetle—he carried his carapace on his back because it was part of who he was again.

The wind picked up, forcing the boat backward as the sharks swam ahead of us. The water rippled around us as little puffs of wind skipped over the water. "Turn to the right, they are over there!" Narutomi said, changing his hold on the mast from his left to right hand. The fisherman pushed the tiller sharply to the left causing the boat to turn, but a sudden gust caught the sail and swung it behind Narutomi, knocking him in the water.

We heard him scream as he fell in, but we were wordless for several seconds as we tried to figure out what

to do. The sail was now flapping uncontrollably in the onrushing wind.

"Get your heads down!" the fisherman yelled at us as he pushed the tiller hard to the right, but the sail didn't move. It had gone too far around the mast, and was now lodged there until the boat came about, which it couldn't do with the sail stuck in that position.

"Help!" we heard Narutomi scream, but we couldn't move the boat toward him. His armor weighed him down, and he couldn't make any headway toward us. We were fixed in our places, he floundering in the water, the boat becalmed and the fisherman unable to steer it. We watched, helplessly, as the sharks bore down on Narutomi.

I saw the first one to reach him bite his right arm off, which disappeared in an instant shorter than it now takes me to tell you. Three other sharks soon had his other limbs in their mouths, and the tug-of-war among them made his armor-encased body shake like a rag doll.

The dark blue-green sea was now red with blood. A late-arriving shark engulfed Narutomi's head in his mouth, and that was the end of him except for the undigested torso in the armor he had so proudly worn, but which had hobbled him, rather than protecting him.

"Well, let that be a lesson to you two," the fisherman said as he got the boat moving again by turning away from the wind. "You have to be very careful when you go fishing."

CHAPTER 15
A NEW MASTER

The fisherman dropped us off at an inlet on the Korean coastline, then turned around and headed back with nothing more than a "goodbye and good luck." We were then all alone, Mori and I, in a strange land without food, weapons or means of transport.

"I never thought we would end up like this," Mori said.

"I wasn't planning on Narutomi being my master, so I never imagined I would follow him once we got here."

"How are you going to find your father?"

The question set me back for a moment. I had gone too far in my assertion, since I would have looked to Narutomi's protection—however insubstantial it might have been—if he'd made it with us. Now, without him, we were as vulnerable as I was the day I left my parents' home, before I joined his little band. I had been too cocky.

"Well, let's stick to the roads until we make it to a city, then ask where the war is."

Mori burst out laughing. "Yes, that's a good idea. 'Excuse me, we're looking for the army that's invading your country. Can you tell us where they might be found?'"

I realized the absurdity of my thinking. "Well, what do you suggest?"

"I suggest that we keep low to the ground, and avoid contact with others. We will learn soon enough where the fighting is."

I agreed with Mori—he seemed to have grown in strategic thinking now that he was the senior member of our bedraggled little cohort.

We set out on the road once again, a tiresome task perhaps, but it was good to feel solid ground beneath our feet. We took our time, allowing others to pass us, hoping to catch a snatch of conversation that would reveal where the Japanese forces had gone. We had the few coins that Narutomi had given me as recompense for the slap he had given me, but it would only be enough to feed us for a few days. We would have to find work at some point, or turn to begging to survive.

The parade of humans and animals that passed by us made for a spectacle of variety—humble carts, rickshaws for the wealthy heading into and out of Pusan, mules, donkeys. We were able to eavesdrop on many conversations, and some travelers spoke to us. We understood what we heard, and were able to engage in conversation with those whom we met, because the languages of Japan and Korea are very similar. We learned that, while the country may have been invaded, life went on as usual for most. Crops and animals grew and were consumed or carried to market to be sold. Babies were born and nursed, and cried when they were hungry. People grew old and hoped to die peacefully, and not by a sword.

We found we could cadge a meal from time to time by collecting firewood, and it was by this means that we fed ourselves as we made our way toward the city. We took our time—one false step and our journey of so many miles, and so many months, could end badly. We did not want to be sold into slavery or impressed into the service of a Korean master.

One day a wagon—what we would call a *kago* in Japan, but which the Koreans called a *gama*—came abreast of us carrying a *hwarang,* a warrior comparable to a samurai in Japan. Mori proposed that we offer ourselves as pages to him, but I resisted. "We could end up fighting against our own people!" I told him.

"We can leave him when we find the field of battle," he said. "In the meantime, it is better to be training as a warrior than picking up sticks in the forest."

I considered what he said, and reluctantly agreed, although I was not so confident as he that we could simply escape whenever we wanted to. Warriors had horses, and we did not. "All right, go talk to him."

Mori ran after the *gama,* and hailed the warrior, whose name was Ho Sik Pak. I caught up with them after they had stopped, but hung back and let Mori do the talking.

"We offer ourselves to your lordship," Mori said.

"Are you Japanese?"

"Yes."

"What is your training?"

"We have learned to fight with bamboo swords. We can ride and care for horses. We can cook, and fetch water and firewood," Mori said.

"Can you bear my *gama*?" Ho asked. "My porters grow tired over long distances."

Mori looked at me—I screwed my mouth up as if to say, "I don't want to, but if I have to–"

"I suppose so," Mori replied.

"Good—I want to stretch my legs. You can take over on the next leg of the journey."

Ho got out of his litter and raised his arms to the sky, then placed his hands on his hips and made the vertebrae in his back crack loud enough for us to hear. "Travel is so tedious," he said. "I envy those who carry me—at least they get exercise."

Ho was well dressed and well groomed, an aristocrat whose perfume preceded and followed his footsteps, like a cloud that hung perpetually over his head. He made for a sharp contrast with Narutomi, who, while he tried to adhere to the samurai's code of cleanliness, could never overcome his frequent falls to *ronin* status and manage a presentable appearance.

"So—you two are warrior cadets, huh?" Ho asked with a look of amusement on his face.

"Yes," Mori replied. Ho looked at us skeptically.

"Is Japanese your native tongue?"

"Yes," we replied with enthusiasm.

"You are eager to be spies?"

"Yes."

"I think it would be an exciting—if dangerous—calling. It requires the cunning of a fox, not the ferocity of a tiger."

Mori and I looked at each other, then he spoke. "We can be cunning."

"All right then. If you help carry my *gama* to Pusan, I will see what can be done."

I looked at Mori with excitement, which was dispelled immediately by Ho's commands. "Take hold of the back rails," Ho said, but when he got in, we could barely move them off the ground.

"What's the matter?" Ho called out jokingly from within. "Aren't you full-grown retainers?"

"Maybe we could lift one rail between us," Mori said. I moved over to his side of the vehicle, got my shoulder underneath the rail, and pushed up with my legs, lifting it off the ground with his help.

"All right, you can relieve my men one by one, we don't have far to go."

As it turned out, Ho was right about the distance we had to travel, but the burden was nonetheless a hard one to bear. Because we were shorter than the grown men who held the other three rails, we could not use our upper bodies and instead had to carry our corner of the litter up high, making it more difficult. When we at last arrived at Ho's walled compound in Pusan, we were exhausted, our hands blistered, our shoulders sore from bearing his body and the litter across rocky roads, uphill and down. He, on the other hand, appeared refreshed, even invigorated by his trip, as he stepped out the door.

"Travel is wonderful," he said as he placed his arms around us and led us up to the threshold of his home. "It really broadens the mind."

An old woman came out to greet Ho, and it was clear from the embrace she gave him and the words that she said that she was his mother. "I have missed you so, my only son," she said, and there were tears in her eyes.

"I have missed you too," he replied. "But I have brought you two presents—see here!"

Saying this he extended his arm toward us in display, as if we were curiosities he had brought back from a foreign land.

"Who are they?" his mother asked.

"They are Japanese boys who have somehow made it to our country, and have offered to become my pages."

The old woman looked us over with an appraiser's eye. She didn't exactly smile, but her face at least registered a receptiveness.

"Put them to work with whatever you have to be done," Ho said. "I have a plan to use them to spy on the Japanese invaders."

"They are too young to cross enemy lines," his mother said.

"Their youth will serve as camouflage. Who would suspect that two young boys were secret agents of a foreign state?"

His mother seemed skeptical, but she graciously ushered us into the house behind her son, who was clearly the sun and moon of her universe. "Take this corridor to the kitchen; they will feed you there," she said. "I will have a bed prepared for you."

Mori and I became part of the Ho household, like stray dogs found on the road who become pampered pets.

"Can you believe it?" Mori said to me as we tried out the bed with clean sheets in the room that we were assigned to.

"It is like a dream," I said. "After all the miles we have

walked, and the hardships we have endured, to fall into this featherbed of luxury!"

A maid appeared at our door. "Come—it is time for hot bath!" she said, or commanded rather.

Mori and I looked at each other, and gulped. "Uh, me first," Mori said and got up.

"No come, only one bath. I am not drawing two baths for ragamuffins such as you—come!"

Mori followed the maid. I stood up and walked behind him into a room with a sunken bath filled with steaming hot water.

"Take off your clothes!" the maid barked.

I did my best to conceal my groin from her, turning away from her view, but she approached me rapidly with a stern expression on her face. "What are *these*?" she said as she pointed down at my badger underpants.

I blushed, but her anger provided a diversion from the more damning fact that she might have noticed. "Those are made from the skin of a badger—to combat lice."

"Disgusting!" she said, averting her eyes and contorting her lips as if she had tasted something sour. "I need a stick to dispose of them!" And with those words she left the room and I was able to get into the bath without detection of my sex.

Mori and I scrubbed ourselves with sponges—we were old enough that the maid did not consider it her job to wash us. We dried ourselves when we were through and dressed in fresh clothes that were brought to us. No one was the wiser.

It felt good to be clean after so many months on the road, bathing only in ponds and streams without soap. I had forgotten the pleasure of scents and soothing oils on my skin. I could get used to this again, I thought.

"I am going to go look around," Mori said. "Do you want to come with me?"

"Do you think you should go out without permission?"

"Everyone seems nice. Why wouldn't I?"

"We do not know our role here—I would wait until we are instructed."

"I am going," he said decisively. "You can stay if you want."

"I will remain here," I said as I lay back on the bed. He left the room, and I fell into a deep sleep, the slumber of a weary traveler who has finally come to rest in a place of comfort.

CHAPTER 15
WE BECOME SPIES

"Get up, Tada!" I opened my eyes, disoriented at first, and saw Mori leaning over me. "It is dinnertime."

It took me a few seconds to remember where I was, and how I'd gotten here. When I was reoriented to my situation, I sat up, propping myself with my arms.

"Where have you been?" I asked.

"All over. There is a stable with fine horses. There is a koi pond."

It all seemed strange to me. Yesterday we were tramping along a dusty road, tired and hungry, after having been dumped on a beach. Today, we were clean, sheltered and about to be fed.

"Where are we eating?"

"A servant is waiting outside."

I got up quickly on hearing these words, and collected

myself. "I am ready," I said, even though I was still groggy from my nap.

Mori drew the door panel aside and we went out into the hallway, where a manservant stood waiting, expressionless. He led us down a corridor to a large room, where Ho and his mother were already seated at a long table. The servant directed us to take places on one side, closest to the door. We bowed to our hosts, and sat down.

"Welcome," Ho said, and his mother nodded slowly, as if she were falling asleep. "You look like you need fattening up a bit."

"We will eat well," Mori said. He told me afterward that he had been advised to say this at the commencement of the meal, and also to wait until Ho and his mother had first eaten.

We sat and watched Ho and his mother dip into a fish broth, raise their heads, and smile with satisfaction. We took this as our signal to begin.

The food was good but more importantly there was plenty of it for the first time in many months. Instead of eating the scraps that Narutomi left us from the modest repast he could afford, we ate heartily. I had to remind myself to slow down so that we would not exceed our hosts in the speed at which we ate. At one point I nudged Mori in the ribs with my elbow to convey this point.

"What?" he asked with annoyance.

"Follow the elders' tempo. Don't wolf down your food so fast."

Mori looked up and noticed that Ho was eyeing him with an upraised eyebrow, as if to second what I said.

"All right," he said, and reduced his teenaged boy's rate of consumption to something less like that of a starving man.

When the meal had concluded Ho cleared his throat and began to speak in a more formal tone to us. "You are probably wondering what I have in mind for you."

"Yes," Mori said respectfully. "We are eager to learn these things."

"As you may know, my country is beset by invaders from your country. I do not know what brings you to our shores, but a guileless youth can be a useful instrument when it comes to espionage. Do you know what that word means?"

Mori and I looked at each other. "No," I said.

"The invaders have hidden in the hills, but we know where they are. What we *don't* know is where they plan to attack next. It could be anywhere. Do you know how to play *paduk*?"

"I haven't heard of it," Mori said.

"It is like the game of *go* in your country. If I could know your next move, I would win every time, but I am not a mind reader. War is different from a board game—any move is permitted. So I want you to find out where the invaders will move next."

"How will we do that?" I asked.

"We can take you by horse to a point outside the forest where the invaders are hiding. We will have to exchange the fine clothes you are wearing for rags again, and you will tell them that you have . . ." Here he thought for a moment, calculating the telling of the tale most likely to deceive our countrymen. "Tell them you were kidnapped by Korean brigands in the Sea of Japan, and brought here to be slaves. Tell them you escaped and wish to return with them to Japan when they have defeated The Righteous

Army."

His mother interrupted him. "You assume the happy ending of the tale that fate has yet to tell you."

"Right," Ho said, then began again. "Tell them you escaped and seek their protection."

"Then what?" Mori asked.

"Then, live with them. Follow them where they go. Get close to their leaders, listen to their consuls of war. When you know enough to undermine their strategy, return to us."

Mori took a deep breath and spoke. "That is a very daunting mission you have laid out for us. What if . . . we do not think we are up to the task?"

Ho's mother spoke. "It is a matter of complete indifference to us whether you live or die. If you do not do as we wish, we will flay you and feed you to dogs."

I gulped, and I heard Mori do so as well.

"Do you think we have fed you, sheltered you, taken you in from the high road, cleaned you and clothed you for diversion?" Ho said.

"All right," Mori said, and nodded his head in submission. I followed his example.

"I am glad we understand each other," Ho's mother said. She stood up, signaling that the meal was over. Ho followed her example as the second eldest person at the table. We stood up, waited until they had left the room, and then departed the way we had come. The life of comfort and ease we thought we were beginning had come quickly to an end.

CHAPTER 16
REUNITED WITH MY FATHER

There followed several weeks of training in the tools and techniques of espionage. We were given Korean-sounding names to give to strangers who would ask us to identify ourselves, so that our Japanese names would not cause suspicion on the part of natives who we might encounter. We were sworn to secrecy about the nature of our mission, and warned that a terrible fate was suffered by spies who "turn coat"—that is, go over to the Japanese side. We were told horrifying tales of torture that were intended to scare us into loyalty to Korea, although I thought to myself that if I went over to the army of my country, I would have their protection, and so this was not so frightening to me.

We were taught which local plants were safe to eat, and which were poisonous. We were given survival packets that including fishing line and hooks, and flint and steel to start fires.

"How far will we have to travel to find the . . . invaders?" Mori asked, checking himself to refer to our countrymen as the Koreans did.

"They are somewhere on Jangsan Mountain. It is not too high, the trees provide cover to conceal their movements," one of Ho's lieutenants said.

"Then . . . how are we supposed to find them?"

"That is for you to figure out."

We spent several nights in the woods near Ho's compound because his subordinates feared that we were too young to have much experience living in the wild. Of course, the opposite was true. Having spent many nights under the stars during our trek across Kyushu, we knew how to fend for ourselves in mountain and forest. We were not the green recruits we appeared to be.

After we had satisfied the espionage corps as to our wilderness skills, we were taken by horse-drawn cart to the base of the mountain and given our final instruction by Ho. "Let stealth and cunning be your watchwords," he said. "Affect at all times an aspect of innocence. You are lost children—appeal to them for protection. When you have learned enough, take your leave and return. Do you understand?"

"Yes," we said together as we nodded respectfully.

"Thank you for the good you have done for us," Mori said, bowing low.

"All I ask is that you repay me with fruitful labor," Ho said, then commanded his driver to depart.

Mori and I looked at each other, overwhelmed by the prospect of the task before us, but not afraid of the mountain with its dense forests.

"We might as well get started," Mori said, and we took off up the first trail that offered itself to our footsteps. We didn't get very far before one path branched into two, one wrapping around the mountain to the right, the other heading in a more direct line to the summit.

"Let's take the high road," I said.

"I say we should go around the low way," Mori said. "An army in hiding is unlikely to climb to the top of a mountain, where they would be trapped. The summit is for those who want to see the view, not those who seek temporary refuge. If you climb all the way to the top, you consume more resources, grow more tired, and then have only one route of escape."

Mori's thinking seemed correct to me, so I agreed and followed him.

We wound around the mountain for some time, seeing nothing of interest other than a black snake that raised its head out of a pile of leaves.

"They are not poisonous," Mori said, "but you still don't want one to bite you."

We crept by warily, and from that time on watched where we stepped very carefully.

We climbed a low ridge that ran above a little rivulet between us and an adjacent rise and my gaze was drawn to the sound of the water trickling below. I looked—and saw a dropline!

"Mori—look!"

"What?"

"Someone has been fishing here!"

He turned and saw what I had seen—a few floats in the water, a line visible at the creek bank.

"You're right," he said. I started to walk down to the stream, but he stopped me. "Better to stay up high, where we can see rather than be seen."

I realized he was right. He began to walk in a crouch, and I instinctively followed his example, although after a few steps I began to feel silly doing so. "We are looking for our countrymen," I whispered. "Why are we slinking like cats?"

"We don't know if that's who we will see first," Mori whispered back. "It could be anyone. If we do encounter the Japanese soldiers, we don't know that they will believe our story."

He was right, so I again began to walk low to the ground, my back bent, my head up.

We climbed higher on the ridge, which grew steeper the closer we got to its peak. Once we were there, we sat on one side, from where we could see both down below in case the fishermen came back, and over the top. We caught our breath and collected ourselves.

"What should we do?" I asked Mori.

"I say stay here and watch. Whoever set that line is bound to come back."

I agreed, but I was thirsty. With all our preparation we had neglected to bring a *wain sukin* (wineskin). From the Korean warriors' perspective this was not an oversight, as *hwarang*—like samurai—travel light and get their water from streams they find along the way.

I made my way down the hill carefully, so as to make as little noise as possible, but walking on dry leaves and sticks made it inevitable that my movements would produce sound. Still, when I reached the creek bank, I saw no one around, and bent over to drink in its cool water. I sipped once, then twice, and dipped my hand down for a third drink when suddenly I felt a hand on the back of my neck, restraining me the way a mother cat bends a kitten to its will.

"Who are you and what are you doing here?" I heard a voice say.

"We mean no harm," I said, and regretted it instantly.

"Who is 'we'?" the voice—that of a man—asked gruffly.

"I mean 'I'."

"There is someone else," the voice said, "find him!" From behind I heard the sound of another scurrying off.

The hand on my neck pressed me down forcefully.

"Ow!"

"Tell me who you are, and how many there are of you."

"We are Japanese youth. We are unarmed. We were taken captive by Koreans but escaped." I realized as I said this that by telling this story, I had not left my options open. If my assailant was Korean, I was doomed.

Instead, I felt the pressure on my neck subside, although whoever was behind me kept his hand there for the moment.

"They have found another!" another man said in a hushed tone, and I could hear the rustling of leaves down the hill that meant Mori too had been captured.

In a moment we were face-to-face again, failures in our attempt to conceal ourselves, but surrounded by natives of our homeland.

"You say you are Japanese—how do we know that?" one of the men said.

"My father is a samurai—Kimiko Kiyotaka."

Two of the men looked at each other skeptically, but a third said: "How would she know that if she wasn't his daughter?"

"The Koreans may have brainwashed her while they held her captive," said one.

"There is no harm in bringing one of them back to camp to see."

"Kimiko Kiyotaka is not my father," Mori said, "just hers. Take her to see him."

The three men thought for a moment, glaring at us through narrowed eyelids. "Stay here with the boy," the leader said. "Don't let him escape. We will take the girl back to see if she is telling the truth."

One of the men grabbed my arm and started to hustle me back up the hill. I turned and said goodbye to Mori—it was the first time we'd been separated for months. He had been just a foolish teenage boy when we first met, but he had grown in my eyes into a mature companion I could depend on.

It was a trek of about three *li* (about a mile) to the camp of the samurai. They had chosen a spot close to one of the mountain's many falls, which provided them with water for cooking and washing; also, the roar of the cataract falling onto rocks below concealed the sounds they might make. I walked with the men in a submissive and obedient fashion—until I saw my father.

"Father!" I said, breaking into a run.

He looked up from the fire he was tending when he heard my call.

"Tada!" he replied more loudly than caution would advise.

"No—it is me, Chou!" and said as I leapt into his arms, tears welling up in my eyes.

"What are you doing here?" he asked, and I told him

the sad story of our family's fate—how I was all that was left for him, and he was all I had in the world. He hugged me tightly, and I eventually stopped crying.

"We will get home again, I promise you," he said, holding me out at arm's length and looking me in the eyes with grave sincerity. "First, we have battles to be fought here."

"I can fight with you."

He looked at me now with a different expression. "You may have disguised yourself as a boy to survive, but you are not a boy."

"But I have been trained as a samurai."

A soldier passing by heard me and laughed. My face reddened, but I was in no position to respond—he was a full-grown man, and a warrior with a long sword. I was just a girl.

"Where? When? How?" my father asked, and I told him *most* of what I had been exposed to as a page to Narutomi.

"You trained with a long sword?" my father asked, still skeptical.

"We trained with bamboo swords, but I learned much strategy, and many useful cuts."

My father's eyes retained their skeptical gaze, but he stepped back and his body assumed a posture of openness. "Show me what you have learned," he said.

I looked around for a stick of the right length to serve as a mock sword, and my father did likewise. When we were thus armed with our mock weapons, we squared off against each other.

With his longer arms my father had a natural advantage over me, but I went through the motions of swordplay in a competent manner. I struck at him from below, as this was the path on which my short stature gave me my greatest advantage. I scored a few touches, which drew derisive sounds of approval from the other samurai, who had gathered around to watch.

"Pretty good, Chou," my father said.

"Her name is 'Chou'—like 'butterfly'?" one of the watching warriors asked.

"Yes," my father answered.

"She indeed does float under and around you, like a young butterfly."

I smiled at my father, but I knew not to be too proud. We had been taught to be humble at home, and to respect our elders.

"We will see whether we can put your skills to use," my father said. "Your mother would never forgive me if you were to die in battle."

"She would never forgive *me* if I had not made the journey here to join you," I said.

My father put his arm around me. "We are both right. Let's get some food in you," he said as he led me toward a fire where a pot of rice was cooking.

"I came here with a companion," I said. "He needs something to eat as well."

"We will send for him," my father said, and he directed the man who had brought me from the creek to go get Mori. I sat down with my father and the other men and told them what we knew, and the nature of our mission.

"The Koreans know where you are, more or less, but they don't know where you plan to strike them," I said.

"For now, we have no plans," one man said. "We withdrew to this mountain because we had fought to a standoff with the Koreans, and needed to regroup."

"We need to move by night," my father said. "We are in enemy territory, and do not know the land as well as they do. Stealth is essential if we are to prevail."

The men talked of attacking the compounds of *hwarang* warriors, and how success in this type of battle would be more likely, and more fruitful, than open combat by day.

I could not disagree, and yet I wondered—why were we fighting in such a dishonorable fashion?

CHAPTER 17

A NIGHTTIME RAID

Mori arrived in camp shortly after I did, along with the rest of the scouts. I explained to him that we had luckily been captured by the very men we were looking for, and his face was at first flooded with relief, then he looked about him with eyes of wonder.

"*Real* samurai!" he exclaimed.

"Unlike our former seven-times-ronin master," I said, with quiet pride in my father's noble status.

"What are their plans?"

I told him the strategy that our countrymen had chosen. "Will we be allowed to join them on these raids?"

"I don't know. They seem skeptical of me, perhaps they will hold you in higher regard because you are a boy."

"You told them?"

"My *father* is here!"

"You didn't *tell* me that," Mori said, mocking my emphasis.

"Anyway, it is not a secret so you can stop pretending."

Darkness had fallen, and the chirping of crickets filled the silence of the night.

"I hope we get into battle," Mori said.

"Wait until you hear their plan."

"What is it?"

"They attack the houses of the *hwarang* at night."

"What is wrong with that?"

"You could end up killing women and children, just as my mother and brother were killed."

"That was a crime—this is war."

"What's the difference?"

Mori said nothing at first. "The robbers who broke into your house were trying to take your valuables."

"As I understand it, we are trying to take land from the Koreans."

Again—silence. "With the robbers at your house, the killings were not their first intent. Had there been no one in your house, they would have taken what they wanted and left."

"If the land of Korea was empty of people, we would just take the land and wouldn't be killing anyone."

Mori seemed stumped. "You had better watch that kind of talk," he said finally. "It is disloyal to your father's cause."

"If it were up to me, he would return to Japan with me now, instead of fighting over land that is of no use to either of us."

"Well, *I* want to get into battle."

"It will not be much of a battle to break into a dwelling

at night and cut off the head of a sleeping woman."

Mori just grunted and rolled over to go to sleep. I, however, was wide awake. It seemed to me that neither path of the two that lay before me was desirable. If I was conscripted into service—probably as a lookout, or to kill those who tried to escape from the samurais' attack—I would be with my father but might be killed or injured myself, or see him die. If I was left behind, he could be killed or taken prisoner and I would never see him again, never know his fate. My long and difficult journey from Japan would have been for naught.

These worries filled my head but finally, by concentrating on a single star overhead, I fell asleep. I dreamed of a return to my homeland with my father in a large junk, not the little fishing boats that had carried me here. We stood in the bow, the wind in our faces, smiling as the sun rose over our homeland. Then, in the dream, someone tapped me on the shoulder. I turned around in that twilight realm between dream and waking and saw my father—in real life—standing over me.

"Chou," he said.

"Yes?"

"Wake up."

"What time is it?"

"It is the Hour of the Tiger"—between one and three o'clock in the morning.

"What is going on?"

"We are leaving for a raid," he said.

I rubbed my eyes—Mori woke up. "Can I come?" he asked.

"I don't think so, not yet. We need everyone to be in harmony, and you have just arrived here."

"You're leaving us alone?" I asked.

"No, a guard will stay here, to watch our food and supplies."

There was a subdued clatter in the camp, as the samurai put on their armor and their helmets as quietly as they could. It had been a long time since I had seen my father in full battle array, and I must admit—he looked splendid, and fearsome.

"We will be back before dawn, get some sleep," he said, then bent over to kiss me.

"I will try, but it will be hard, thinking that you might not come back."

"I will be back—we choose our targets carefully."

The warriors took off down the mountain in a single line, hardly making a sound. The wind was blowing and the sound of the branches of the trees stirring provided cover for the little noise that they made.

I pulled my blanket up to my chin and rolled over to try to go back to sleep. My eyes had only been closed for a few moments when I heard rustling sounds coming from where Mori lay.

"What are you doing?" I asked.

"I'm going to follow them," he said. He was rearranging his blanket on top of some sticks to make it look like someone was sleeping underneath it.

"You're going to get in trouble!" I said.

"Don't worry, I'll be back here long before them."

"How do you know?"

"I will keep at a distance, far behind them. I will have a head start back up the mountain."

"Don't do it, Mori."

"Why not?"

"Because if you disobey orders, they won't trust me either."

That caused him to pause, but only for a second, and he stood up to leave. "Why should I worry what they think of a girl?"

I hit him—hard—on the side of his head. "Don't you say that to me after all we've been through. I've kept up with you every step of the way from the very beginning."

He rubbed his head—I don't know if I'd hurt him very much, I think he was more embarrassed than injured.

"I'm going, Chou. You can come with me if you want, but you're not going to stop me."

I took a deep breath and looked around for the guard. He was sleeping—we could hear him snoring over the chirping of the crickets.

"All right," I said. "But we're turning back at the first sign of danger."

"Why?"

"*We don't have swords, stupid!*"

"Oh—right. Well, we'll just have to conceal ourselves well."

"You'd better, otherwise I will have inscribed on your tombstone: 'He is completely concealed today, because he was not well concealed in life.'"

We slipped out of the camp and headed down the hill. The warriors were now far ahead of us, and we could only guess at which direction they had taken when we came to a fork in the trail. There was moonlight, but we stumbled more than once.

After a while we reached the base of the mountain, but we were still far off from any dwelling.

"Mori, let's turn back, we have too far to go and we

don't know what we are looking for."

"You made me bring you, don't complain now," he said as he plunged ahead to a field of grain.

We were exposed by the moonlight, which cast eerie grey shadows beside us as we trotted along. When we reached the edge of the field we came to a road, and along its length a few houses.

"I'll bet they attack here," Mori said. "We can watch in safety from the bushes."

We hunkered down to watch and wait—and wait, and wait. I fell asleep at one point, and Mori had to nudge me awake. But no amount of waiting could have prepared us for what we saw as the Hour of the Tiger came to a close and the Hour of the Rabbit (from five to seven in the morning) approached.

We saw them before we heard them, walking in close formation as before, but this time not with an air of stealth. No, they came toward us with a bounce in their step, and as they drew nearer we could see that some of them carried—severed human heads!

"Oh my!" I gasped—I could not help myself.

Mori, on the other hand, was fascinated by the spectacle. "Wow!" he said, his mouth wide open in wonder.

Once all the samurai were past, our next step wasn't clear. It was all I could do to stop Mori from rushing to join the passing samurai. "Don't," I said. "They will be angered to find that we followed them."

"Well, we can't stay here."

"We should follow them at a distance. They know the way, and if we are attacked, we can call out for help."

We shadowed the samurai back to the camp. Our

heads barely reached the top of the grain in the field so we had no difficulty concealing ourselves when we needed to. The hard part would be to find a way to circle around them when we neared camp so we could reach there before them, and not get in trouble for sneaking out. I was tired, and was having trouble keeping up with Mori, who seemed excited and energized by the sight of blood and gore.

"Mori, slow down!" I called out and as I did so, I tripped over an exposed tree root. I landed flat on my belly, barely breaking my fall with my hands, but more important was that I lost sight of Mori and the returning men. I was alone, exposed by the moonlight, unsure of how to get back to camp.

I kept my head down and cursed Mori as I made my way across the field, hoping I could make it to the foot of the mountains before pursuing Koreans saw me. I heard an outcry at the border of the field where it met the road, and knew that I had very little time.

My pursuers were a long distance away, but they were joined by a man on a horse who could be heard galloping in my direction. I thought it best to hide in the hope that he and the others would pass me by.

Unfortunately, I hadn't counted on the *jindo* (dogs). They sniffed me out as easily as they would have found a deer, and a pack of three surrounded me, barking and baring their teeth, leading the men to where I was.

The Koreans approached and examined me.

"Who are you and what are you doing here?" a man on horseback asked.

I could not say that I came from the camp, for that would lead them to my father. "I . . . am lost," I said weakly.

"Where do you come from?"

"Pusan," I said. It was the only town whose name I knew.

"You are a long way from home. How did you get here?"

"On foot," I said. "With my brother. We are orphans."

"Where is your brother?"

"I . . . don't know. We . . . lost sight of each other in the dark."

The men on foot had now joined the rider, who pointed to me with his short sword. "Take her back with you. I will press ahead."

"What should we do with her?"

"Feed her, put her to bed. She says she is an orphan and separated from her brother."

At first, the men on foot looked at each other with puzzled expressions, then one stepped forward, called off the dogs and taking my hand, pulled me to my feet. "Come this way, little one," he said. "There are marauders out tonight."

CHAPTER 18
I AM A CAPTIVE

Long afterward, Mori told me what happened when he got back to camp. The men had already arrived, and my father was distraught to find me gone.

"Where is Chou?" he asked, frantic.

"We followed you down the mountain," he said, still panting.

"So, where is she?"

"I . . . don't know. She fell behind on the way back."

"And you didn't retrieve her?" one of the other men asked.

"No," Mori said, and hung his head in shame.

"This is not the Way of the Samurai," the man said with disappointment in his voice.

"We must retrace our steps and find her," my father said.

"You go, and you," the leader of the samurai said, pointing to the man who had spoken. "The boy stays here. We must prepare to leave in a hurry, they will be pursuing us now."

With that, my father and the other warrior took off down the hill, flying—I'm sure they knew—into the swords and spears of those who were pursuing them. A clash between the two was unavoidable.

I, on the other hand, had been put to bed by the Koreans and was as clean and comfortable as I had been back in the Ho Sik Pak's compound. A matronly woman—the aging mother of one of the soldiers—had fed me, drawn a bath for me, given me a clean nightgown and led me to a quiet room in the back of her house. As much as I tried to maintain consciousness to plan my escape I could not, and I soon fell into a deep sleep from which I did not wake until the sun had risen to a mid-morning height in the sky.

When I appeared for breakfast the old woman was gracious but reserved, as she had been the night before. She suspected nothing, but was nonetheless curious as to how I had come to be lost in a field in the middle of the night.

"Your parents—did they live around here?" she asked.

"No, we lived in Japan."

"Then how did you get here?"

"In a boat."

"Obviously. You could not fly with the birds. Whose boat?"

"A fisherman."

"Why—were you fishing?"

"No, he was. We just wanted to . . . come to Korea."

"What happened to your parents?"

"They drowned in a storm."

"And the fisherman brought you here anyway and just left you on the shore?"

"Yes, grandma."

I could tell that the old woman was not convinced but still, I was just a harmless girl. She had no reason to be concerned. Her son returned later in the day and told her that there had been a skirmish in the moonlit field that night, but that the invaders had escaped and his side had suffered no injuries or fatalities. "What have you found out about this one?" he said without aggravation.

"She says she came to Korea in a boat with her brother, their parents died in a storm."

"She is Japanese?"

"Yes."

The man came up close to me and looked me squarely in the eyes. "Why would your parents bring you to Korea in the middle of a war?"

I lowered my eyes, as I could not bear his stare. "I don't know. Maybe they didn't know about it."

"Well, we have to figure out what to do with you." He conferred with his mother for a while, and apparently they agreed I should remain there for the time being. The *hwarang* was about to leave when there was a commotion outside. When he opened the door, I saw one of his fellow soldiers in an agitated state.

"Is there a young girl here?" he asked.

"Yes, why?"

"Is she Japanese?"

"Yes—why do you ask?"

"She is apparently with the invaders. They are looking for her."

The *hwarang* rubbed his chin with a look of cunning on his face. "What are they willing to give for her?"

"I did not ask."

The *hwarang* thought for a moment, then spoke. "Tell them if they leave our land, they can have the girl back."

I felt my stomach turn at his words. I did not want to be the cause for an ignoble retreat for my father—I could not think of a greater shame.

"I will convey this to them," the man at the door said, then left.

The *hwarang* gave me sickening smile and said, "So, little one—you are now an item to be bargained for." He laughed with coldness in his voice. "Keep her inside, do not let her wander about," he told his mother. "I will post a guard at the door, so she cannot escape."

And so I became a prisoner of war, in nonetheless comfortable surroundings. I had food, an accommodating if unfriendly hostess, and a warm bed at night while I waited to be reunited with my father.

There followed a succession of tense but uneventful days. I helped the old woman with household chores as directed, but otherwise kept to myself, waiting for something to happen, I knew not what.

And then one night as I was lying awake, unable to sleep, I heard activity outside the house. The sound of men with heavy treads, accompanied by dogs, caused me to sit up in bed. The hour had come.

The door to my little room burst open and it was the old woman's son. "Come with us," he said, and I got up and followed them outside.

We tramped through the dark with just a single lantern to guide us, returning to the field where I had tried to hide from them. We took a few steps into the grain, then the *hwarang* and his men stopped. "Go ahead, slowly, the dogs and I will accompany you. When they reach the point where they found you, they will stop. Someone from your country is to meet you there," he said. "If there is more than one, or if any of them are armed, the dogs will set up a howl, and the arrows of my men will rain down upon all of you. Do you understand?"

I gulped, then nodded.

"Proceed."

I stepped gingerly ahead, walking behind the dogs with only the muted light of the lantern to guide me. Every now and then I would trip across a root, or jump when I stepped on a fallen stalk that I thought was a snake.

Eventually we reached the spot that the dogs knew from my scent and they stopped, as the *hwarang* had foretold. The dogs sat back on their haunches, lifted their ears in anticipation, and waited attentively for whatever might emerge from the woods at the foot of the mountain. Eventually I could make out a few glints of light coming toward us. It was, I realized once my eyes had adjusted to the sight, samurai armor, shining from the reflected glow of the moon overhead.

I squinted, but did not move. I did not know what orders the *hwarang* had given the dogs. With each step the samurai who had been sent as the emissary of the Japanese took toward me, the clearer his features became until I realized—it was my father!

I resisted the urge to run to him, but could not keep myself from calling out to him.

"Silence," the *hwarang* ordered, and I became still again.

My father advanced slowly, his hands at his side and not on the hilt of his short and long swords. When he was within, say, ten paces of us, the *hwarang* called out "Halt!" and my father stopped.

"This is the girl," the *hwarang* said. "Is she yours?"

"Yes," my father said, and I do not think the *hwarang* understood how this was doubly true—I was both Japanese *and* his daughter."

"Then take her away."

"I will do so."

I started to bolt toward my father, but the *hwarang* placed his hand on my shoulder and stopped me. "Leave your long sword for me," he called out.

My father hesitated just a moment, then moved his hand to his scabbard and drew out his sword. With a slow and deliberate movement he drew it out, then held it with one end in each hand, as if to show the *hwarang* that he could do him no harm with it.

"Toss it on the ground, far from you," the *hwarang* said.

My father did as he was instructed, giving his weapon a little push with his hands to propel it away.

"You may go," the *hwarang* said to me, and I ran to my father's arms. "Now back away—both of you."

We stepped lightly, lifting our feet high, as we could not see where we were going.

"That's far enough," the *hwarang* said as he swooped down and grabbed the sword. "Now—leave, and never come back!"

The *hwarang* stood there stiffly, his dogs at attention, as we turned around and made our way back to the mountain.

CHAPTER 19
A DOLPHIN SMILES AT ME

Whatever wrath and punishment I had earned for disobeying my father was thankfully muted by his gratitude for my safe return from the Koreans. He had never been a demonstrative man, but he hugged me tightly as soon as we were out of the range of the dogs and the *hwarang* who had led me to the spot where I had been exchanged for a long sword.

"Are you all right?" my father asked once we entered the forest at the base of the mountain.

"Yes, I was not mistreated. I was well fed."

"Good. Mori told us that it was his idea, but still . . ."

"I know. I am sorry."

When we reached the camp, the samurai were preparing to leave.

"Where are we going?" I asked.

"A truce has been called. We fought them to a stalemate, but we are low on provisions, while they can live off their land."

I could see the disappointment in my father's eyes, and hear it in his voice. He was without a long sword, and also without a foe to lure him onward. While I yearned to return home, I did not like to see him unhappy.

I went to the place where I had left my blanket and saw Mori. He apologized for getting me in trouble.

"It's all right, I guess. My father is not angry at me, just glad that I am safe."

"Well, we will have great tales of adventure to tell our friends when we get back to Japan."

I started to agree, but then it struck me: I didn't know what had become of my friends, nor would they know what had happened to me, I had taken off so abruptly. And Mori? As I understood it, he was probably worse off than I was, having been on his own longer.

"Where will you go back to?" I asked him.

"I will go back to my parents in Hishū," he said, and I could tell that the prospect of returning to the home that he had left in search of adventure did not appeal to him.

"What will you do?"

"I suppose my father will apprentice me to someone. Perhaps a blacksmith."

"You could learn to make swords!"

"I would spend most of my time making horseshoes," he said.

"That doesn't sound so bad."

"I suppose not. At least I would be around better horses than Piebald."

He realized that he had touched on a subject that was

sensitive for me.

"Sorry, I did not mean to denigrate Piebald—he was a good horse."

"He was. But I suppose his time had come."

The Hour of the Rabbit was coming to an end, and the Hour of the Dragon (seven to nine a.m.) was beginning. We headed down the mountain, and as we emerged from the cover of the trees we saw the sun rise over the water, a glorious sight but one that I was almost too tired to appreciate.

My father noticed me lagging behind and came back to help me. "You are too old and too big for me to carry the way I used to when you were a baby," he said.

"If I could only sleep for a little while . . ."

"We have no time to stop. I will put you in the cart." He called to the teamster to stop, then he boosted me up into the cart, where I lay down on top of a bag of rice that was the expedition's only remaining sustenance.

I promptly fell asleep, and was woken with the smell of the salt air from the Korea Strait in my nostrils.

"C'mon, time to get in the boat." It was Mori, lightly shaking my shoulder as he spoke.

"Did I sleep all the way from the mountain?"

"Yes, lazybones."

"*I* was out all night, unlike you."

I clambered out of the cart and made my way down to the shore, where Japanese boats awaited us. Mori, my father and I got in one of them, and—when the tide was at its flood—we caught a land breeze coming down from the mountain and headed home.

I went up to the bow of the boat to get some wind on my face and wake up. I squinted into the rising sun above

Japan, and exhaled. I closed my eyes and, when I opened them, saw a pod of dolphins alongside us. They looked happy, and I thought—easy for them.

But then I reconsidered. They had their enemies, too—sharks and fishermen, among others—so their days could also be troubled by strife.

Still, they survived, even flourished—or at least they *seemed* to—as they swam alongside us. They kept pace with us, mindful of the dangers they faced, but content with their lot.

I smiled down at one, and I thought I saw her smile back at me.

ABOUT ATMOSPHERE PRESS

Atmosphere Press is an independent, full-service publisher for excellent books in all genres and for all audiences. Learn more about what we do at atmospherepress.com.

We encourage you to check out some of Atmosphere's latest releases, which are available at Amazon.com and via order from your local bookstore:

Newer Testaments, a novel by Philip Brunetti
American Genes, a novel by Kirby Nielsen
All Things in Time, a novel by Sue Buyer
The Red Castle, a novel by Noah Verhoeff
Hobson's Mischief, a novel by Caitlin Decatur
The Black-Marketer's Daughter, a novel by Suman Mallick
The Farthing Quest, a novel by Casey Bruce
This Side of Babylon, a novel by James Stoia
Within the Gray, a novel by Jenna Ashlyn
For a Better Life, a novel by Julia Reid Galosy
Where No Man Pursueth, a novel by Micheal E. Jimerson
Here's Waldo, a novel by Nick Olson
Tales of Little Egypt, a historical novel by James Gilbert
The Hidden Life, a novel by Robert Castle
Big Beasts, a novel by Patrick Scott
Nothing to Get Nostalgic About, a novel by Eddie Brophy
Alvarado, a novel by John W. Horton III
Whose Mary Kate, a novel by Jane Leclere Doyle
An Expectation of Plenty, a novel by Thomas Bazar

About the Author

Con Chapman is the author most recently of *Rabbit's Blues: The Life and Music of Johnny Hodges* (Oxford University Press), winner of the 2019 Book of the Year Award from Hot Club de France. His work has appeared in *The Atlantic, The Christian Science Monitor, The Boston Globe*, and a number of literary magazines. His young adult short story, "The Vanishing Twin," appeared in the March/April 2015 issue of *Cicada*.